KU-631-056

Days

327861

Days

EVA FIGES

FABER AND FABER
3 Queen Square
London

First published in 1974
by Faber and Faber Limited
3 Queen Square London WC1N 3AU
Printed in Great Britain by
Latimer Trend & Company Ltd Plymouth
All rights reserved

ISBN 0 571 10455 X

© *Eva Figes 1974*

For my daughter

1

I recognize the room: although it is still dark. I have been lying
in it for several days. It is not quite morning yet: the window
at the far end of the room, facing my bed, gleams faintly. It
seems so distant because I cannot reach it; in fact it is a small
room. The walls, now shadowy, are smooth and white. There
is one door, not visible now, in the righthand wall, just below
the end of my bed. My arrival has been blotted out: I cannot
remember it. I suppose I must have been pushed through the
door by somebody.

Having recalled my surroundings, I am calm once more.
After a moment of panic. During which, having opened my
eyes from one darkness only to find another, my breathing
seemed very fast, and I felt a strong urge to scream. Sweat
soaked into my nightgown, which has since stuck to my skin.
It is all right now. I am calm. Listen to my breathing, how
regular it is. In: out. In: out. It simply took a moment for
everything to sort itself out and register. For the faintly
gleaming square to become visible, a window. For me to
disentangle who I was, this body in which I am possessed, a
particular body lying in one room, a specific bed, the walls
surrounding me.

But now I am reassured. I know that I have nothing to fear.
All particular things are like that: limited. One knows where
one is. It is a small room in which nothing much could happen,
furnished with clinical sparseness. Since nothing much can

change now I expect it will not take me long to get used to sleeping here, to the shock of waking. I remember once, as a child, staying in my grandparents' house and waking up in the small hours, in a strange room, unable to account for a black shape nearby. I went through a whole range of possibilities, remembered the room as it had looked by lamplight the evening before, but nothing fitted the black mysterious bulk which waited, without moving, for me to know it. Unidentified, it continued to threaten, it might still, at any moment, move. Was it possible, I thought hopefully, that tomorrow was my birthday, or some other special occasion I had somehow managed to forget? I lay for what seemed hours in fear and expectation. Now I think of it, dawn must already have been breaking, since enough light penetrated for me to see something. When my grandmother finally drew back the heavy hangings it was neither delightful nor sinister, merely an item of furniture which had always stood there.

In this room there is not much for me to know. It is small, rectangular. In the days I have already spent here I have noted everything there is. I doubt whether there is anything left which I have not taken into account. And since I have nothing to occupy my mind, since I lie here incapable, I have also measured the walls and detected minor flaws: a long hair-crack in the ceiling and, round the lightswitch, a dark penumbra no doubt caused by the many hands which have rubbed against the wall whilst turning the light on and off.

If I could only stay awake, if only the night could be pushed back indefinitely. That is when the trouble starts, after dark. Once the day has been terminated and I am delivered back to the womb of the dark, lying alone with my thoughts. Then the data so carefully sorted and arranged to make sense becomes jumbled again. I do not know where I am, or who. The walls, so carefully constructed to protect me, fade away, leaving me exposed, disorientated in incalculable dimensions of darkness. Choking in twisted passages, hearing sounds. Tomorrow, if I wake, I shall have to start all over again, at the beginning.

8

Putting up the walls, making things tidy.

Counting things, adding up. Even now, fully awake, I feel I am lying in a fishtank: the walls moving, luminous in the shadows, my head crammed with dreams. I am dangerously exposed.

Of course, I know I can put it right. That is what the conscious mind is for. Now I am fully awake I can put back the walls. I know where objects belong even though it is still too dark to see them. There is a washbasin to my left, attached to the wall. White, solid, and curved. If I listen hard, perhaps holding my breath as I do so, I would no doubt hear a slight hissing sound coming from the tap. The washer needs replacing. Or the nurses are careless about turning it off tightly. Or both. I listen: hear nothing. And remember my dream.

I know this hospital also has public wards. Perhaps this knowledge, listening in the dark, conscious of the building as a massive honeycomb, single sounds coming through spaces, perhaps this caused the walls to fade, in spite of my request, the wished-for privacy. I was aware of bodies breathing, turning in the long dark area, coughing coming from humped bed-clothes concealed behind flimsy screens, groaning in their sleep or fearfully awake. Staring into the dark. I know what lies beyond, well enough. But now I want my walls back. It should not concern me. Not now. I have myself to think of.

It did not take long. After that initial moment of panic. Once I had opened my eyes, blinked away the confused stuff spilling out of my brains, accepted the dark. Once I had placed the walls securely back where they belonged, round my person. Exist, followed by I. The knot of nerve ends looking out from the bedclothes. After that it does not take long to come back. Previous days come back to mind and modify me. Continuing to exist, I conclude: I still exist.

I am not unhappy. My situation being what it is, I concentrate on its limitations. I am, after all, not required to go any

9

further. Or act on my own behalf. Time will take care of things, or at least bring destruction. I am not going to allow myself to sit and judge between good, better and worse. I have carefully avoided questioning the doctors about the prognosis. Time will tell. I do not want to know. Meanwhile, it is rather soothing, since I am lying quite comfortably. I suppose I shall develop bedsores after a while, if this continues, but for the moment I am lulled into a sense of cosy security, like a second childhood. Nothing can happen to me.

And yet, in some curious way, I feel it is possibly deliberate. It has all come so pat, been accepted so passively, that I somehow suspect myself of a deliberate plan. At moments I sense this: that such passive acceptance is not human. It amounts to an action, if I could only comprehend its topsyturvy logic. At times I tell myself I have come to avoid a conspiracy, the pitfalls that waited (and still wait, all round the building) to lure me to my destruction. The outside world is full of such pitfalls. I suddenly got an uncanny intuition about it, though I have never seen them, never even suspected them before, and I knew with absolute certainty that to move forward, in whatever direction, was to go under, violently, in some appalling manner. The entire physical forces of the world are poised against me, ready to hurl themselves in my direction.

If, for instance, I was to walk out now, supposing I was able to do so, I think I should undoubtedly pass straight under the huge oncoming wheels of a bus. Rattling heavily through the murky premature dark, this oncoming vehicle (lorry or bus) might perhaps flash its lights or hoot a warning, but no attempt to apply the brakes would be made. Not, at least, until it was too late.

So it is just as well I am unable to walk.

I try not to think about it during the day, concentrate on this curious relationship with my body and the ritual of hospital life performed round it, but there are occasional reminders, too obvious to ignore. The room is not soundproof, for example. During the day most of the noises which come through to me consist of activity in the corridor immediately outside my door: the arrival of food, instruments clashing on metal, voices, the whine of the lift. But during the night, after the day staff have left and there is not much activity, I become aware of the city outside, its hum, increasing beyond this quiet place. The city never sleeps, it grinds on, churning, all round the hollow shell in which I am lying now. Terror runs through it, the walls vibrate, concrete shakes to its fragile foundations. Earth tremors. The machine goes on moving, all wheels turning, in spite of anything that could happen, individual loss, suffering, death. It is this knowledge which is too much for me: that nothing will bring it to a stop, however momentary. I lie listening in my hollow of darkness and know that it will ignore my death just as it has so far failed to acknowledge my existence.

I used to lie awake before, many nights. Not just in this place. There are certain things one cannot accept. But though the nurses bring you pills here I refuse to have my mind wiped out. That will come soon enough. I used to lie awake, waiting. It was such a quiet suburban road, after midnight one could hear single sounds quite clearly, footsteps crunching gravel, a milkbottle overturned, it rolled down two steps. Dark spaces soon become filled with images. A cat howling for sex. Boys out late, whistling, laughing. Catcalls. I listened for the sound of his car turning into the drive. The engine would die. I waited, knowing the sound would not come, or not for ages, knowing also that I could not rest until then. Rage filled me, hatred, as I hit the pillow for comfort, finding none. How could he, knowing I would be lying like this, waiting for the sound of his key in the lock. And the knowledge that he could, knowing this, was the worst of all.

I was young then, that was my trouble. Foolish and impressionable, head full of impossible ideals, notions which did not include the thought of betrayal, the guideline of lust. I did not realize that nobody ever comes home.

My body tossed and turned on the bed, trying to wear itself out. To sleep one needs to be exhausted.

Now it is still. Deprived of movement, but still aware. Waiting, though in spite of itself, and without hope.

It seems built into the organism: hopeless hope. Without it perhaps not only movement but also consciousness would cease. Perhaps. When the night nurse came round I refused the chance of immediate release, a paper cup holding two white pills. Instead, I was very cunning, since you never know when conditions might become intolerable. So I picked up the glass of water from my locker and pretended to swallow them. Later I hid the two pills, still tucked into the palm of my hand, under the pillows.

As it happened, I dozed off soon afterwards. Found myself inexplicably back in the open ward, listening to the various forms of unease, discomfort, difficult breathing, footfalls of nurses, whispers, at any moment now the steps would break into a run, disturbing everybody except the one in the corner, now intent on dying. His breathing relayed to the wakeful by the latest contraption designed to prolong the agony. The difficult intake of oxygen a harsh sound made meaningful by growing pauses, the final pause an open parenthesis with sister already trundling the cylinder away.

I could, it occurred to me, begin hoarding the pills in my locker.

I moved through the shadowy, subdued spaces and came across a face I had not seen before. She was sitting up in bed with a puzzled expression on her worn face, unfamiliar to me, she looked bewildered, but I recognized the bedjacket round her shoulders. I had made it, with that scalloped pattern, for my mother many years before. The doctor stood close behind me, whispered in my ear. He was taking me on a tour of the hospital. She has been offered the pills, which was what she was thinking about. Obviously we like our patients to take the long, slow, hard way, because that is what we are trained for. But legally we are obliged to give everybody freedom of choice. Finally she looked up into the doctor's face. He was standing nearby. No, she said. She spoke hesitantly, with a frown on her face, unsure of her own decision, not wanting to be misunderstood, regarded as a coward. I'm expecting a visitor. I wouldn't like him to come all this way for nothing.

Visitor. Nobody has come. The room waits in the dark, a rectangle, rather like a fishtank. The chair intended for a visitor, should he come, stands, though I cannot see it now, because it is still dark, below the window, a little to one side, with its back across the far left-hand corner.

Had he come, he would have been able to face the person in the bed, resting his hands on the curved wooden arms which run, tense as a bow, strung between back and seat, attached to the upholstery. The hospital staff would, I think, allow the chair to be drawn closer, should this be desired, thus permitting a holding of hands and intimate glances, the expression of concern. But so far nobody has come.

I wonder what the time is. It cannot be far from morning. How slow the hours seem when one is wakeful, only waiting for morning. Too late now to take the pills, I should be found comatose, which would arouse suspicion. My condition might even be misunderstood, the wrong treatment given. But I find it hard, now, to control myself. Keep a guard on my thoughts. I want so desperately to keep things simple, but the walls waver, things come in on me. In the dark the fish floats, hardly moving, warily he keeps his eye wide open in the dark, always on the lookout for danger. But there is no escape, and wariness is not enough. He is unable to close them, since he was born without lids. One night he made a courageous leap: I found him lying breathless on the window ledge the following morning.

The window gleams. Faint light, bluish. But this gives me no clue. It might be the first light of dawn but in the city night is never total, utterly black, nor do birds sing. In our suburb the houses stood in rows with overgrown gardens lying back to back: awake, I heard the dawn chorus many times. It meant good-bye to hope of sleep but also freshness, a new day with the sun coming over the rooftops. Now traffic begins to thunder round the concrete bastions, black rivers of asphalt, and the only dividing line between night and day will be the flick of an electric switch. The buildings are too high, too close together to watch dawn coming as the earth turns heavily. It is winter anyhow, it will be dark for hours yet, long after the regular morning routine has begun.

Because it is a routine.

I like it that way. It makes me feel safe. The faintly disturbing, luminous square on the far wall will be blacked out, the walls will be shown for what they are, flat and white, at the turn of a switch. Tidy, clinical, and suitably two-dimensional. As the time-table is followed dreams will be blacked out by the smooth lighting, forgotten. That is how I want it, not this, not the long hours with my head expanding, an empty space, a curious receptacle full of holes through which anything can float in, disturbing thoughts, memories. The voice, for example, I heard a voice. What was it saying? So close to my head that the air moving could have tickled my ear. But I felt nothing, so I suppose it must have been in my head. I have forgotten the words, so why should I still feel uneasy?

I must make an effort and fill the empty spaces with images of my choice. It is the only way to keep the bad ones out. Such as primary colours, and picture books. A bright red boat with fat white sails bouncing over the water. And the pretty waves. White clouds being blown across the blue sky. Darkening and turning to rain. I shiver, having come out unprepared. Perhaps we should turn back. Already the wind is turning my flesh to goosepimples, driving through my thin shirt. It was a mistake to have come.

No.

Sunlight through eyelashes, iridescent, the light refracted as through a forest. Heat burning me brown. A smell of oil. A taste of ripe fruit pulled out of the paper bag and eaten, one by one. Juice running down my chin. Stones buried in sand.

Small stones, very very small. Each a jewel. The miracle of sand. I am crouching under a bush, sniffing my knee. Somebody is calling for me, because it is time for supper and bed, but my hiding place is safe. A small black bird hops quite near, I hold my breath and watch it, as it perhaps regards me: sharp head held inquisitively to one side, listening. The eye blinks. Its thin claws hop off over the damp brown earth, scattered with small stones of various shapes. I see the image still.

It has gone. Did it register anything of me? I stayed behind and wondered. Finally I crawled out from under the bush because nobody had come to fetch me. I was getting cramped in that position.

Nobody has come. It must be still official night. The window gleams, lighter now, just enough now for me to distinguish the jagged outline which I know to be a branch. At the best of times I cannot see more than this, can only assume the whole tree, guess its type, it being winter now, and leafless. It may even be dead. Perhaps I shall find out eventually, if I have to lie here long enough. For the moment it looks black and gnarled, bent like an old man's arm, with a knotted elbow.

The tap is hissing slightly, I am sure of it now. If I hold my breath and concentrate I can just hear it. It sounds like a gasping windpipe, almost a death rattle, eerily prolonged. But I cannot stop breathing for long enough to make comparisons. We used to try it as children, and always ended up gasping, red in the face, having lost the fight with the life force inside us. It made us laugh, then. Our lungs bursting, we burst out laughing at an impulse we could not understand, but did not give breathing much thought.

But I heard a voice. I remember now. I lifted the telephone receiver and, after the ringing sound in my ears had stopped, there was someone, a man's voice trying to get through, only I could not make out what he was trying to tell me, it was a bad line, a pneumatic drill began to thrum deafeningly outside my window, what, I shouted, could you speak a little louder, not knowing even who it was, whether it was someone I already knew. For all I knew it might be a stranger, a wrong number, who knows, someone I did not like, but I hung on desperately, trying to hear his words. When it was too late everything suddenly went quiet.

I wish I could move. My back and buttocks ache from lying in one position. How long before the bedsores begin? I am also sweaty and sticky. My skin prickles. I feel hot. I push my hand under nightgown and an odour of sleep, of warmth and body, escapes. I feel first one breast, then, with more difficulty the other. Both are round and soft to touch, unexpectedly so, I am astonished at the ripeness under my palm. I thought they had already shrivelled away like last year's fruit, leaving only wrinkled skin and hard dry nipples. Perhaps if I were to run the tips of my fingers along my face, following the outline of nose, brow and cheeks, this would also now, feeling in the dark, be as in memory. The photograph album. I shall resist the temptation. Touch is a deceiver. It could serve no purpose, not any longer. But already my index finger has found, is following, the line of my chin. I must stop.

That was not all. I remember now: I must stop it, I thought, standing by the upstairs window, in the dark, but not quite dark, the dim hush that comes just before dawn, watching the old house burst suddenly into flames, brilliant colour growing in the dark, rising, licking at the woodwork outlined now, about to be consumed, nobody seemed to be stirring, asleep as before, afterwards, watching the gabled roof blazing, the rows of similar houses still black, unaware, I saw a figure run out towards my door, knock, why mine I thought but went below to answer, a woman with distraught hair, gasping, a smudge of soot across her face, pushed something into my hands. She was elderly, her arms knotted, skinny under the working overall. I thought, she said, you might like to have this. It was only after she had gone that I recognized the greying, broken object in my hands as an old doll of my child-hood.

It was quiet afterwards, ashes falling on ashes, piling up quietly in my head, blocking up the orifices, rather like snow. Grey snow. Black snow. Nobody had come to help. The doll had only one arm, its eyelids were scratched off. Nobody had sounded the alarm, but then, it had all happened so suddenly. I could not understand why she had come to me, the woman, although the battered old doll had certainly been mine.

Dark is soothing to the eyes. Above my head the ceiling floats, a slab of concrete. The lid of a tomb, except that I cannot read the inscription on the other side. Still, what do dates matter. I am safe here, nothing can touch me.

I can hear traffic now, outside, begin to gather momentum, accelerating towards morning, working hours. But it has nothing to do with me. All day I shall lie here, doing nothing. If I could block the sound also, I would do so now. I heard it in my bedroom from the main road and knew it was time to get up. The house was silent, and cold. I went downstairs in my dressing-gown and filled the kettle. I knew he had not come back. I went into the boy's room and had difficulty in rousing him. He kept withdrawing under the bedclothes. Hurry up, I said. You'll be late for school.

Silly dreams. In fact I remember nothing. Things are sorting themselves out now, in a comfortable blank. Soon the nurse will come and take charge. Meanwhile I lie here, re-signed, listening to my own breathing. I think the staff find me a good patient. A lot of people, particularly in the public wards, think they have been brought here against their will, under false pretences. They grumble, make things difficult for the nurses. There is no pleasing them, either they are not getting well fast enough or the hours are passing too slowly. Meanwhile their relatives are selling off their possessions. They have nowhere to go.

I am different. I accept the routine. Rarely ask questions. I lie here quietly and accept at their hands, because I know they are doing what is best. I was always good, as a child. Obedient. I always disliked making an exhibition of myself, openly show- ing anger, rage, or hurt feelings. Now it has become easy: there is nothing left to hide.

2

The first section of the day has passed easily enough. Un-
eventfully. I am now laid out, waiting, propped up with extra
pillows, my body washed, hair brushed. The room is a white
rectangle. Four walls. The left- and right-hand walls confront
each other, an identical match. The window opposite is beginning to fade. First it was black, for a while it changed to a
beautiful luminous blue, now it is just an ordinary grey. I
can make out the old man's arm, bare, leafless, cutting across
with its knotted elbow and no doubt, beyond the limits of the
aperture, a begging hand. Suppliant fingers of bony, brittle
twigs, now touched with frost.

I call the window a square but this is an assumption. It is
a belief I cannot verify. I have spent hours of previous days
trying to be sure in my own mind that the vertical and hori-
zontal sides were of equal length. I returned to the problem,
if only briefly, this morning. I have tried swinging an imaginary
ruler across, but I find it hard to keep a firm hold on the end
meanwhile, and since it is imaginary I cannot be sure that it
does not change to fit on the journey. Hands have a habit of
doing this too, so even if I could, being able to get out of bed
would not help. They move towards the desired conclusion.
Regardless of reality.

The message I found in his eyes was one I had been
looking for.

The grey window, square or not, promises little or nothing.
A dull day, wintry. Unremarkable, like all other days. I
imagine that the sky above the building is now heavily over-

cast. The whole city lies under a blanket of unbroken cloud. Soon drops of rain will spatter the pane, singly, afterwards merging. Or perhaps it will pass over, lift and lighten. I do not care. The tree cares, if it is still living. A parched hand, begging for water.

Since my vision is partial I do not even know what type of tree it could be. I expect it is one of several in a small cheerless garden closed in by high walls. I have known such. A place for the occasional patient in a thick dressing-gown, hunched on a bench, blinking palely into sudden shafts of sunlight. A space where hospital staff cross hurriedly from wing to wing, wintry weather catching at capes and starched caps. A place for confidential conversations, for bad news to be broken in private, and then discussed. Private affairs, professional sympathy. Holding you by the elbow, whilst you forget everything but the touch of his hand on your elbow and the message you read in his eyes. He had no idea, probably, of the harm he was doing.

I merely think this. In actual fact I can only conjecture about what lies beyond the walls of this room. And in the last analysis it does not matter. I no longer allow it to concern me.

My body has been washed, the hair brushed. The distasteful bedpan routine has been forgotten, not entirely perhaps, but almost. The nurses are young, healthy. I think they exude a scent of soap and disinfectant. They have to be strong and athletic in this job. I picture them, a few years back, not much more, playing hockey for their school with proper enthusiasm. They are consistently tactful, do not pass judgement on my body. Any comments are favourable. What pretty hair you have, one remarked, having taken my brush and comb out of the locker drawer. I smiled, for her sake. She set about grooming me with the intensity of a child who had been given a doll with implanted hair.

Afterwards I lay back, waiting. It was still dark outside. Now people would be stumbling out of bedclothes, yawning, fumbling for slippers, switching off alarm clocks, going down to put a kettle of water on to boil. A heavy lorry drove past nearby, and my bed began to vibrate. Opposite, now brightly in view, under the electric light, the chair stood waiting. Somebody had now begun moving through the day towards it.

A cup of tea stands on the locker. I have allowed it to grow cold, after only one sip. It does not interest me. The cup looks familiar: its shape has been repeated many times, stood on thousands of surfaces. There is a small chip in the rim, and from it a crack runs down the side. I am told that such a cup should be thrown away, since chips and cracks in the glazed surface allow germs to settle. Now that the liquid has cooled a whitish skin has collected on the dark surface.

Hospitals should know better than to serve tea in imperfect cups.

I took a cup to his room and allowed it to stand there, all day. When he came home in the evening he would know, seeing the cold tea with its congealed surface, that I had come into his room and found the smooth surface of the bed, unoccupied. He took me for a child. Now he would know I was not ignorant.

So I was prepared for adult life. I stopped being childish. Long before it happened to me I knew about waking in a deserted house, running my hand through the empty half of the bed. In my mind I saw a procession of naked women, pendulous breasts and tousled hair, but little of their faces. Small flats, bedsitters, rumpled sheets smelling of lust, twitching with sex in the early morning, fumbling in the unfamiliar bathroom for the light switch, looking for a razor. Going to work in yesterday's shirt.

The cup stands, untouched. It is a continuing reproach to the living.

Coming back I could not tolerate her pained expression, perhaps the reason why I changed her face, wanted the doctor to give her something. It was inconvenient that she had made the wrong decision. Nobody was coming to see her. I was confronted with a silly woman who would not understand without being told, refused to accept her own redundancy. I was left with her puzzled expression and the burden of dealing the fatal blow. So instead I wove an elaborate web to protect her, hung it round her shoulders. I spent hours knitting an intricate pattern, my guilt compounded of pink wool and difficult stitches.

I was not going to resemble her. I would go through life with my eyes wide open. Knowing what's what. I already knew a thing or two.

The room is white, almost, and brightly lit. I find it reassuring. At first the light flickered for an instant as though a thunderstorm was about to break, I found it slightly disturbing, this sharp division between night and day, but now we have both settled down. I have freedom to study my surroundings, unequivocally, without motive. I am calm. The old woman who brought my tea, on the other hand, wore a slightly pained expression, as though her body, probably her feet, could not hold out. She had to get up at five every morning, she told me. This morning it had been dark still, and spitting rain, and she had waited twenty minutes before a bus finally came. It was getting too much for her, nowadays, spending so many hours on her feet. Her husband had been disabled, hanging about the house all day. And her daughter had been a right fool, marrying the wrong sort, walked out and left her a couple of months back, and her with four kids.

The untouched tea is liable to upset her. She may feel her work has been all for nothing, when she comes back. But I cannot bring myself to swallow it, although I would like to, for her sake.

I take in as little nourishment as possible. To swallow requires effort. Sometimes it also produces nausea. And as I am simply lying motionless all day I require little food. Unnecessary bulk only produces unnecessary and excessive excreta, which I dislike. I loathe the humiliation of the bedpan. The smell and discomfort. One lies afterwards, soiled, longing for a hot bath. Microbes move from the skin surface and become embedded in the surrounding fabric. Nurses are not forced by the daily time-table to do anything about such secret disgust.

The time-table is strict, beginning long before official sunrise. The nurses work hard round the clock, on and off. This allows the problem to be subdivided into a number of easily understood tasks, after basic training. Each task must be ticked off, since the highly organized rota and the large number of problems, patients and tasks makes it unlikely that anyone will remember what they did to whom the day before, if, indeed, they ever did. Thus the machine is not only kept fed and functioning, but monitored for error. Urine is collected, measured and analysed. The behaviour of blood corpuscles is carefully studied, and at intervals during each day pulse rate and body temperature are checked and recorded on a chart which hangs at the foot of the patient's bed, forming a graph through time and space which only the patient cannot see.

The nurses carry gadgets in their breast pockets. Which bulge. Scissors, large round watches with speeding second hands galloping round the face. One junior has a small egg-timer which she holds to the light. I am full of admiration for their devotion to duty, though I cannot at present see how this will change anything. Or help me.

Still, I am glad of their attention. I want them to continue to be kind to me. I like the tone of voice in which they speak to me, the way my physical needs are all catered for. Although my heels and buttocks are sore from lying so long in one position, a nurse will soon come to massage them and relieve the ache. For this reason I was anxious not to be misunderstood when the two pills were found. I had forgotten all about them when one rolled on to the floor during bedmaking, the nurses had been standing, one on each side of my bed, plumping the pillows, normally discussing their own affairs above my head, but during a short silence it could be heard quite clearly, hit the floor like a popping button, and roll. Whereupon the second pill was immediately found under the pillow. The two nurses glanced at each other, conscious of a serious mis-demeanour. One turned her attention to me. Sister would have to be told. Heaven knows what she would have to say. She sounded censorious, as though I had wet the bed. I could not think what to say in my own defence, not before they had both left the room.

I am afraid of sister. I do not know what she will do, when she comes on her round. She may withhold my letters.

She may report the matter. She has the ear of the doctors, and the hospital authorities. She usually comes in, each morning, after the breakfast things have been cleared away. She is a large woman, wearing a dark blue uniform and a starched, buttoned collar. She stands by my bed, middle-aged and virginal, reminding me of a strict nanny, or a head-mistress I once had at primary school. She looks down at me to say a few words. One hand cradled on the other as she talks, not saying anything of consequence, only how are you, which is not so much a question as an assertion, you definitely are, and to qualify this would be mere niggling, a sign of ingrati-tude. So you say nothing, except to smile and say thank you. A tall, solid woman, with a curiously ample bosom, bearing in mind that it never suckled babies. Its function, if any, is purely part of the whole, a figure of authority. In her hand, the one propped up by the other, she holds letters which have that morning been sent to the patients. Stamped, freshly franked with wavy lines and a date, her thumb obscures the name written on the first envelope, the one facing you. She gives no hint, no clue, simply makes the odd remark, always the same, about it being a good morning, and passes on to the next room. Am I, you wonder, being punished? Am I being taught a lesson?

I am helpless, I know that. I have to rely on the kindness of others, since I cannot walk out of this room and look after my own needs. I would soon starve to death if the hospital staff did not do their duty. Inconceivable perhaps, but they could certainly make life very uncomfortable for me without

24

endangering themselves. I know from childhood what it is to be helpless. And hopeless too, now, in this solitary room. Without a future to look forward to. Not that this is ever voiced: such a defeatist attitude would instantly arouse indignation. It is their policy to encourage patients to think they are improving, particularly if they are about to die. The staff disapprove of death, it is the enemy who must never be mentioned. So we all go on pretending, playing our game.

I will try to go on pretending, sticking to the rules, being so very helpless. When sister comes round I shall smile, and somehow show how anxious I am to co-operate. I must, above all, make it clear that I had no intention of committing a misdemeanour when I hid those pills. That I respect everything they are doing for me. That I simply had no need of the pills when I pushed them under my pillow. I was not, in fact, trying to hide anything at all.

A fly has settled on the rim of the cup, which still stands on the locker by my bed. Balancing on its crooked legs, wings flat, it moves forward, round the curve. Now it has apparently found the place where my lips touched and drank, it has stopped, appears to be taking nourishment from some thin, invisible skin. Flies carry germs, death on their feet, but I bear it no ill will. It was, after all, custom-built for a purpose. Its wings are strangely beautiful. It goes through life, single-mindedly fulfilling that purpose. I only wish I could do the same, but I have no idea what that purpose is, for which I might have been born. If there is one.

It is not the sort of thing people want to discuss. But I wish I could catch somebody in the right mood, because I should like to talk about it. But everybody is always so busy, and then, each person sees me differently. The foreign woman who comes in once a day to sweep the floor thinks I exist in this place to make dust. The elderly woman with her puzzled expression and troublesome feet believes I am here to consume her tepid, unpleasant tea and perhaps bring about her own untimely death. The groomed, grey-haired consultant who comes in once or twice a week knows I am here to prove his expertise. The last time he came round he was almost angry because I had so far not conformed to his expectations; no doubt he will wash his hands of me if I fail to confirm his prognosis, do not respond to treatment. As for the young girl who comes here with her hopes, it is her I would like to spare. She brushes my hair, washes me, as though I was the doll she left at home, only recently.

The traffic rumbles, gathering momentum. Just now the building shook.

A shock at that age could be terrible.

On winter mornings the traffic moved slowly, halted, inching forward, braking. A slight fog clung to the atmosphere, visible in a haze round streetlamps still burning. Cars had their lights switched on. A satchel strap digs into your shoulder. The air smells cold, rough in your nostrils, seeping through your clothes and chilling your skin. Slowly the sky has begun to fade. The day has been packaged, prepared for you, you are aware of this as you wait for the bus to turn the corner, the correct number illuminated up front, so you can clearly read it, the route you take each morning. You already know the time-table, but you quite enjoyed the packages, music, languages, art and biology, prepared for you, supposed suitable for your time of life, not all, of course, swallowed the weekly dose of physics with a good-humoured grimace, pretended to be indisposed during games. But loved art, poems, and words. But now it is different, everything has changed. Because somebody waits for me, suffering, hidden wounds which do not heal, stinking, a smell which follows me through the day. The dark unlit house I have left behind lies deserted, unoccupied, a black hollow in the pit of my stomach.

It undermined my concentration.

For the young nurse, willing, eager, I lie in wait like a trap. Her fresh skin smells scrubbed clean, of soap and water. She travels back home for free week-ends, a place of love, security, the source of all she knows. She thinks of me as a task, a job, but I am the source of all she has still to learn. She will not thank me for it.

This is absurd. I do not know why such thoughts should come into my head. I had a bad night, that must be the reason. I seem to recall now, a curious dream, staring down from my bedroom window (always windows, I have spent the most lonely moments of my life staring out of windows, gazing out, long dreary moments, waiting for something, or for nothing in particular) I did have a disturbed, disturbing dream about a small child playing down on the pavement with an outsize doll which lay in a pram, except that it was not a doll, but the body of a full-grown woman, and the body was a corpse, and I knew that it was me. I looked quite young, though I don't know how a full-length body had been squeezed into the pram, slightly pale, with closed lids, dark hair spread, body covered by a white shift. But I knew it could not go on, she was trying to lift the head, to feed it like a baby and I knew, because I had read it in a book, that brown fluid was liable to ooze from the dead mouth. She must be protected, I thought, the little girl with her flat chest and grubby feet in cotton frock and sandals, and I ran downstairs, pushed the body into a shed at the back of the house. Go away, I told her, but I knew that the old shed with its broken wooden slats could only be a temporary hiding place. Rats would come. A smell might arouse the suspicions of the neighbours.

My concern was for the child, her innocence. For myself, I only felt indecently exposed.

I had a bad night, that was it. The mind plays curious tricks. But I am safe now. The room has four walls, clean and white, brightly lit. Aseptic. Window and door help shut out the whole world. Nobody can see me. I am free to study my surroundings at leisure. The light in the centre of the ceiling is a round milky globe which can be conveniently switched on or off to suit man-made hours. You can also switch sleep on and off with chemicals. Nightmares are simply chemical. The moon is redundant now, you have only to walk through city streets after dark to know that. It shines, even in summer skies, a half-forgotten or discarded promise. We have no use for it now even though, secretly, we still bleed each month.

3

It is not a new experience to lie in this position. I have foretold it, somehow. These four white walls have been familiar to me all my life. Various people have come and gone: I have studied their posture and expressions.

The fly took off from the rim of the cup and began to weave round the room, from side to side, possibly trying to find an escape route. Sometimes I lost sight of it, since it is small, and not only fast, but also unpredictable. It weaves from side to side, trying to find a way out, possibly damaging its sensitive structure whilst colliding with solid walls. Perhaps the only way it has of knowing that such enormous and hopeless obstructions exist. I think I have read that it navigates in relation to the source of light, in common with most small and all winged and flying creatures. This is the source of its desperate confusion. The window is a dull grey and is, anyhow, firmly closed.

It has now settled on the ceiling light. I can see it, no more than a black spot, illuminated quite clearly by the light, crawling across the bright surface. The glass must also be a source of warmth. It crawls to the edge, turns round, walks across the surface once more. Soon it will come to another edge, which is in fact the same one, unbeknown to it. I must look away: I cannot bear to watch it.

A newspaper lies folded on my bed. It was left there by a wizened little man with a bony head. His body looks as though it had been picked up and twisted by a gigantic hand. He now walks with a limp, but does not complain. On the contrary, he arrives regularly each morning with a few chirpy remarks and fresh papers, although I do not thank him, or give him money. I have not ordered the paper: presumably somebody has told him that I used to read this particular newspaper, and thinks I should be encouraged to continue the habit. I never look at it. But each morning I watch for his interesting head, which shows the skull beneath the skin. He grins broadly, showing blackened teeth with wide gaps between. He appears to despise cosmetic dentistry, or perhaps he cannot afford it. Anyhow, I like to regard his teeth, too foul not to be genuine. In this place they are the only real teeth I have seen.

I have not touched the newspaper. I can see printed words and a smudged image which appears to be a photograph, badly reproduced. I have seen such images before. The print attempts to arrange itself in different patterns but after a time it cannot help but fall back into the pattern it had before. I have seen it happen, time and again. I have got tired of being deceived, time and again, into believing that this time the arrangement really is different. It costs too much effort, only to be told what you already knew, how the pattern has started to fall apart again, since the centre would not hold.

Instead I spent the last half hour looking at the jug. It was also brought in, by a foreign woman. I know her to be foreign because she has a dark skin and never says a word. Each time I see her impassive face above the water jug she is carrying into the room I try to arrange my thoughts into words she could understand. During my lifetime I have learnt several languages, inadequately, but now I find myself lacking in courage to try any of them. Surely, I think, some opening phrase which would be understood by her for what it is, a friendly gesture. But I am held back by fear of making a fool of myself, bringing it out all wrong, and suppose it turned out to be the wrong language, I could imagine the expression on her face if she heard what sounded like gibberish. But I think it is the expression on her face which puts me off: it does not encourage confidence or invite friendly overtures.

Looking at that saturnine skin covering a plump fleshed-out face, one might think I did not exist at all. All that exists in her mind is the glass and the water jug, many glasses and many water jugs in various rooms, the doors numbered. Her duty is to clean them.

There are fingerprints on the jug, smeared patches on the supposedly clear surface.

Various people have come and gone.

The chair stands empty, as it has always stood.

A young woman has been, with a row of glass test tubes which rattled slightly in a wooden stand. She was very calm, very professional, immaculate in a white coat, with smooth hair and regular features. Her movements were smooth too, unhurried and measured. She knew what she was doing, being a trained technician. She pricked my finger and sucked my blood out through a thin tube. I watched her and marvelled at the smallness of the pinprick, the delicacy of sensation, the pretty colour of the bright red blood, like a shining bead, which she smeared oh so gingerly on to a glass slide. But afterwards she applied pressure to my arm, the band was so tight I began to breathe fast, to panic as the vein in my elbow swelled, I thought it would burst, finally I watched with disgust as she withdrew a syringe full of blackish liquid, my life was a sluggish thing, thick, dark and heavy, not an underground river, more a stagnant cesspool or sewer. Now being drawn out of me. My head felt faint. I could feel myself getting weaker as I watched it being dredged out by the cubic centimetre, not so much at the thought of being deprived of it, but on account of the reality, its discouraging appearance.

The blood, she said, will be replaced in less than half an hour.

Not meaning, of course, that she will bring back what she has deprived me of. She laughs, twists the rubber tube round her hand, shakes several of the tubes. You can manage that quite well on your own, she said. The body is a marvellous thing. Quite a factory for corpuscles. She is a technician.

Production will be resumed. The possibility of a breakdown does not occur to her. She nods, picks up her equipment, and walks through the door with my blood. The door has closed now.

The chair stands empty, as it has always stood. It has been made with a shape that looks constantly ready to receive somebody, with back and arms to hold. When I look in the direction of the chair I suddenly realize that the hours have dragged, heavily. It has all been a waste of time.

I can hear the traffic moving through the day.

Somewhere there is a young girl, making her way through the day, looking for an explanation. By the time she comes here, probably towards the end of the day, she will not have found one. She will arrive baffled, confused, knowing that what she does know cannot be told. It is too much for the human mind to grasp. It certainly cannot be tolerated by the sick and ageing woman she will have to confront.

She will try to avoid speaking the truth.

Instead she will offer comfort, lies and evasions, knowing that eventually she must come to grips with the truth, the hard facts. And that with each passing day it will become more difficult. She is hoping that delay will make her strong enough to bear it.

I am not ready for it, even though I know the juncture must be soon. I look forward to her visit.

This time she will bring me good news, hope. The hours that have already been spent waiting, must accumulate, bring one nearer final reward. Hours you will not need to live through a second time.

But the window, there has been a subtle change in the window. Difficult to know how, exactly, only that it is different, the light, with time passing, having passed. I feel light-headed, my body weightless. Perhaps because too much blood has been taken out of me.

Imagine how it must have been for her, having it all removed, her function. Nub. Kernel. Nothing now but a husk,

32

for throwing away. She had produced us, we owed her some-thing.

I didn't ask to be born.

All the same . . .

Oh, don't keep on. It's not my fault.

I switched the light on, pulled back the blankets. The room smelled of dirty socks, stuffy. This room stinks, I said, and pulled up the window. Cold air blew in. For God's sake, he grumbled, and pulled the covers back over his head. Hurry up, I said, it's late. I can't do everything for you.

Go away. I could hear his muffled words under the bed-clothes. I pulled them back off. He blinked, rubbed his eyes and yawned. You're worse than mum, he said, rubbing his scalp, the already rumpled hair. I hadn't time to argue with him: You'll be late for school. Get up.

I went downstairs and set the kitchen table for breakfast. Put two eggs on to boil. From his attic window I could see the main road still lit in the dark, the long rows of tall lamps, cars already moving in both lanes. I heard him coming down the stairs.

Where's dad?

He was still yawning. His school tie was crooked. He had flattened his hair with his hand. Just a kid, a baby, who knew nothing about anything. He was maddening, but I wanted to protect him, the remnant of his childhood.

Out.

He was cracking the top of his egg and making a messy job of it, peeling off fragments of shell. Part of the yolk began to run down the side.

Ugh, this is too soft, this egg. Perhaps you'd better go up and wake him. He'll be furious if you let him sleep all morning.

He's out. I told you. He didn't come back last night.

He was bringing his head down to egg level and pushing spoonfuls into his mouth.

D'you mean to say we've been on our own all night?

Yes.

He stared at me, spoon still in his mouth, then slowly withdrew it. A sliver of white clung to his lower lip, dropped to his chin.

I'd have been scared . . . if I'd known.

Well you didn't, and you aren't. So eat your breakfast and go upstairs and clean your teeth. And brush your hair properly while you're about it.

All right. Honestly, you're worse than mum.

Thanks. I notice you haven't asked after her.

Oh well, how is she? She's getting better, isn't she?

Yes, of course. But it takes time. And you might take the trouble to go in and see her.

I don't fancy the idea of hospitals. I wouldn't know what to say to her. I'd be embarrassed.

What, with your own mother?

I know, but . . . I say, d'you think you'd better ring the police or something?

Whatever for?

About dad. He might have got murdered, or been kidnapped, or lost his memory.

I shouldn't think so. He probably had a flat tyre and spent the night with a friend. I expect he didn't ring last night for fear of waking us.

He was disappointed, but already preoccupied with plans for the day. He got up, scraping his chair backwards, licking butter off his fingers. Had I washed his football clothes? Yes, I said, they were in the top drawer. He left me alone in the kitchen. I scraped breadcrusts into the wastebin, tipped out eggshells which crumbled under my fingers, and stacked the dirty dishes in the sink.

He was a bit like a chicken, with his rumpled hair, a chicken which had broken out of its shell. The shell was left behind, useless, hollow, it crumbled under my fingers. I washed my fingers under the tap, a sticky fluid stuck to them, embryo fluid. The dishes would have to wait until tonight. I wanted to atone for what I had done, we had both done, but I could not

34

put back what we had taken out and devoured. The house hung above my head, ugly, deserted, but her life's work. She would want to know that it had not been neglected in her absence, rooms untidy, dust under the furniture, not so much because of the work involved in putting things right later, but because neglect undermined the purpose of her whole life. We were leaving her, all of us, but she must not know. Not yet, anyhow, not while she was still so unwell. Somehow I would have to find time to clean the place up.

He ran downstairs, shouted good-bye, and banged the front door behind him. I would have to go too, now, or I should be late for school.

Tonight I would go to see her.

The chair would be standing empty, waiting for me, facing the hospital bed. She might now be looking at it, face drawn with pain, wondering, why had nobody come? I would have to think of something to tell her, some excuse which sounded convincing.

The window, there has been a subtle change in the window. A gleam of light passing. Now it has gone. From where I lie in this box I cannot see the sky, but I can imagine how clouds would have passed, the momentary gap.

She will be moving through the day. I can see her, in my head. She wants to learn to draw. Her favourite teacher is the English master, a middle-aged man who encourages her. She likes writing essays for him, giving her a chance to express something, if not herself, since she does not know who she is. But something, if only ready-made, expressive of sentiment, sensibility. She would adore her father too, if given a chance. But she has not been given a chance.

Altogether, she will have few chances in her life. And those she will probably fail to recognize.

35

I remember my grandmother, towards the end of her life, occupying a bed in the front room.

I remember now:

Granny had a fall, she said. Yesterday, sitting in that chair. I wish you could come home.

She tugged nervously at the handkerchief between her fingers.

My grandmother's bed had been moved to the ground floor. The curtains were kept drawn, the air was stuffy. A shaft of dusty light streaked across her bed and hit the floor. Go away, she muttered. I want to sleep. She did not know what time of day it was. The room, normally our living-room, was now cluttered with a paraphernalia of bottles, cups and spoons, pillows and bedding. The household routine had been totally disrupted, nothing was normal now. But grandmother could not be moved. Then grandmother would not be moved. Eventually grandmother had to be moved, all the same. It gave us one spare room.

Mother was distraught, which puzzled me, since she had shown no particular affection. She had moved in with us when her own house was bombed during the war, and she never stopped talking about it afterwards, what she had lost in the air raid, how terrible the war was, and the one before that, what a shock it had all been. She disapproved of us, considered us spoiled, not imbued with a proper sense of hierarchy. I did not want to visit her in the hospital. I had never seen a person close to death before, and it frightened me.

Round and round her fingers, she kept twisting the handkerchief, tugging at it.

It started with a fall. This time too. Another step, taken like a thousand others, made through a sequence of so many forgotten days, begun carelessly enough, like all the others. But this one was not to be completed. A stray thought, perhaps, leading to an odd misjudgement of timing, distance to be traversed, though the space, each step and angle, was familiar enough. Or perhaps the cleaning woman had used too much polish. Not removed a patch of grease. The X-ray has not yet come through, but it is almost a foregone conclusion.

Lying here, I can follow her through the day. In my head. She is frightened. She will not be able to cope.

Lying here, I can follow her through the day. She feels tired, because there is too much which has to be done. The days follow each other in relentless clockwork. Today is a particularly bad one, because she is menstruating. At the beginning of a period her body becomes alarming, starting with a slight ache in the small of her back, depression, wanting to cry, becoming angry at the least thing. Afterwards it is as though a pronged iron had been pushed up her, she feels the pressure in her back and thighs, standing in the bus queue, no sign of it, and she is already late for school.

I cuffed my brother round the ear. He did not understand what it was all about, why I was so irritable. That night I forced him to come to the hospital with me. My homework, he protested, I'll get into trouble. So long ago: what, after all that, did he have to say to her?

Someone did come, I remember now. Only now does the resemblance strike me, how like the boy he looked. A man stood here, in this room, with little enough to say, a day or two ago, was it yesterday? The chair waited behind him, standing in the corner as usual, but he would not sit down and lean back, once or twice he perched on the outer edge but at once stood upright again, he was nervous, uneasy, I saw how he paced up and down the room like a caged animal anxious to

37

make his escape. He fiddled with his hat brim, but had not unbuttoned his coat. I suggested : it's very warm in here. Perhaps he did not hear. Once or twice I saw his eyes look full into my face, then I recognized them, something about the pale gold-flecked irises, the questioning expression. I tried to think of something to say, he was trying too, I could see that, but he gave up too soon, turned away. Some remark about it being a nice room, about my surroundings. He glanced at the walls, and finally the door. I could see he wanted to get away, he was of course a busy man with an important job. You've done well in the world, I said. He shrugged: you know how it is.

The day is far advanced now. Outside these walls traffic has risen to a pitch, it has taken off and hums now, an invisible swarm of giant locusts, predators, hovering in the air and making the entire building vibrate to the rhythm of their wings. The breakfast tray stands forgotten on the locker. The egg yolk has congealed hard. It has been standing there for a long time.

Sister has not arrived yet. Perhaps, after all, it is her day off.

I wonder what nurses do on their days off: what they do to leave all this behind.

I hear a noise in the corridor. A broom knocking against the wall, low down, near the floor.

The light still shines in the centre of the ceiling. Nobody has come to switch it off. Wasteful of electricity. But it appears to have darkened outside. Perhaps it is going to rain.

There is an invisible hollow in the day, towards the end of the morning, when everything threatens to collapse.

Nothing to do. The dark sky, the deserted street with heavy

clouds above the rows of rooftops, everything suggested a catastrophe. The entire world has been wiped out, or had taken shelter before an imminent explosion. Plop. The first drop of rain, I hoped by this time the box was safely underground, so that my mother could take shelter from the rain. She had gone to the funeral without me. You've been ill, she said, no sense in your going to catch your death. Drop followed drop, running down the pane. I'll take care of everything, I said, but behind me the beds, still unmade. There would not be many people. My mother had ordered a wreath in my name. I don't know why, since she was hardly likely to read the labels. The house hung round my head, draughty, spacious, full of holes. I had never been to a funeral. Nobody left, she had said, I'm the only one. It was an ugly house, more so for being familiar, the woodwork riddled with tiny holes where it had been cured of woodworm, stained dark to look like oak, so dust always showed up. Full of senseless corners difficult to clean, where you could not get with a dustpan and brush, or forgot, and the whole place was a firetrap, with no way down, especially from the attic room.

Sometimes, in my dreams, I know that I never left it. I am unaccountably back, marked out by my school uniform, setting out the evening's homework on the table. Soon it will be time for supper, then bed. I am afraid of falling behind. Outside the window it has begun to rain. It is getting dark. Water runs down the pane.

I liked the words of the burial service. I sometimes read them in my prayer book. Ashes to ashes, dust to dust. I thought them quite poetic.

I wish, she said, you could bring yourself to throw it away. My mother was talking about his old teddy bear, which had turned from grey to near black with age. It still sat on his bed during the day, one arm missing. My brother slept in the attic room, which always had a curiously stuffy smell, unlike any other part of the house. My mother said it was his dirty socks; she also thought the old teddy harboured germs, was by now disgustingly unhygienic. From his attic window he shot at pigeons with an airgun, and occasionally took potshots at the apple tree which stood at the far end of the small garden. His room led through to the storage space under the roof. It held old trunks, also my discarded toys. Dolls, a doll's cot. I wish, he said, that I could.

The cleaner has opened the door, half opened it. She is beginning to sweep the floorspace of my room, but so far I can only see one shoulder. The rest of her body is hidden by the door, its surface of grained wood.

It was when I brought the baby back that it suddenly got too much for me, the house. I could not bear it. My doll's cot was still stored away in the attic, almost a replica of the one I had bought for her when she was born. Perhaps that was the reason I chose it, standing in the department store, who knows. I had not thought about it before. The first night I put her down in the spare room, stood over her after I had pulled up the dropside, my hands still gripping the edge, and I suddenly thought, what am I doing back here, what shall I do? Her eyes were already closed, mouth busily sucking the fingers she always sucked. She settled down without a murmur that first night, odd that, one of those things, and mother said to me, after she had come in from the kitchen, she's settled down nicely. The wallpaper hadn't changed in ten years, nor the furniture, it still stood in exactly the same places. Even those bits of polished brass she collected still stood where they had always stood, through my whole life. What, she asked, are you going to do? I don't know, I said. And I didn't. All I knew was, I should not have done what I had done, come back here. Yet there was nowhere else to go.

You're a little fool, she said, a while later. She had made us both a cup of tea. The baby was sleeping quietly, but the evening was early yet. I knew the talk had to come. She poured out the tea and began work on the shawl she had been making for her ever since she was born. He's a nice young fellow: you could do a lot worse. She went on twitching wool round her fingers, round the hook. Soon she would be too old for it. Thousands of women have to put up with a lot worse than that. You should be thankful. I didn't want a lecture, not from her. Like you and father, I suppose—no thanks, I'm not hanging around for that. The moment the words were out I wanted to retract them, wished I had not spoken. I had thrown a stone and waited, now, for the ripples, the sound of shattering glass. But it did not come, she did not say a word. Normally my father was never mentioned, a conspiracy of makebelieve was maintained within the house. It was partly my own fault, at the start I had been as anxious as anyone to shield her. Now she concentrated on the work between her fingers, counted loops, held the pattern up against the light. Then she said (still looking at the work, not me): A child needs a father. I'm not saying who's right or wrong, but a child needs a father. You shouldn't take that chance away from her, your own daughter. Now you're being selfish. I didn't know what else to say, sat there brewing resentment. She's better without one, I thought to myself. How I hated my father.

The cleaner is now fully in the room, cleaning out the corners with her broom and long-handled pan. She has moved the chair. A thin, wiry woman with slight curvature of the spine and a hollow chest. Her sleeves are rolled up, showing hard forearms which years ago gave up all claims to femininity. Her hair is tied up in a cloth, but I can see a strand across her forehead. She sees me looking at her and grins, showing a gap between her front teeth. She makes a lot of noise. She does not seem to mind dirt, stirring up dust which gets into her nostrils. Or perhaps she has got used to it, over the years.

One has to. I can smell dust now: I am breathing it up my nose. It has got very dark outside. It must rain soon. I can see only her back as she stoops to sweep under the bed, hear her breathing. It's going to rain, she says, straightening up. What a day. You don't want this tray, do you? I'll take it away. Still, mustn't grumble, they do a good job, these girls. Where would we be without them, that's what I always say. It's tough, and some of them kids are only just out of school. You haven't eaten much. No appetite this morning? Oh well, never mind. I couldn't have done it at their age. All this sickness, dying and death. It's not pleasant. Woman in the end bed died last night. Gave me quite a turn, coming in to do her room and finding it empty. Mind you, she looked terrible. How are you feeling?

I wished she would go. She was getting on my nerves now. I did not want to hear. Why do people have to stir things up? All my life I have hated it, the smell of dust in the air, skin prickling with it, invisible but palpable dirt settling in one's hair. Why does cleaning involve such an upheaval, moving things, stirring things up? Better to let it lie. But she has gone to the door only to place the breakfast tray outside the door. She comes back. She is apparently in no hurry this morning.

She wipes the top of my locker, pushing the empty glass with her hand. My buttocks ache. My eyes have begun to prickle, my skin itches. Her hands show a fine tissue of lines, engrained with dirt.

I could tell she was not long for this world. Poor lady.

I did not answer. She leaned over me to dust the headrail behind me, and I could smell her, so I decided to stop breathing for a while.

Goodness, she said. What a lot of tissues. Scooping up the crumpled remains. Have you been crying?

No.

Oh well, that's good. I expect you're starting a cold. What a nice card, she added, setting it up, the bit of cardboard, beside the water jug. Who sent you that then?

I don't know. I don't remember.

And I did not know. I was not being uncommunicative. Nor did I have any wish to know from whom it had come. It was one of those printed cards that you buy in a shop for a trifling sum. It had a drawing on the front, lightly shaded, of a bunch of flowers. Roses coloured pink, forget-me-nots blue, but nobody had come, nobody had brought them to me, placed them between my hands, squeezed them gently so I would not let go, so I could feel their bulk. Hands had lain on outside for days, when the nurses straightened the top sheet and bed-spread before official visits they picked them up and put them down again, idle and empty. Nobody has come, filled them for me. Instead somebody has sent me a cardboard drawing of roses and forget-me-nots.

My buttocks are sore. I wish somebody would come and do something about it. I could ring the bell but, on the other hand, I would not like the possibly irritated expression and aggrieved tone: now what? I do not want to be considered a nuisance. It is embarrassing to draw attention to oneself.

If I stare hard at the ceiling I can see a blob, like an after-image, from staring at strong light. The blob becomes dis-tinguishable as a cluster of roses and forget-me-nots. On the lid of my tomb. Placed there by nobody I can think of.

I have stared at the light too long. Blinking, the blob begins to swim. If it was not artificial, but the real sun, I would long ago have gone blind. Before leaving the room the cleaner did try to switch it off, but the room then was much too dark. Rainwater ran down the pane. She switched the light on again.

The blob is rapidly removed by blinking, reforms on my vision, a faint mauve shadow that darkens like a fist on the horizon.

So I was not dreaming. I did hear noises in the night, foot steps running, urgent whispers outside the door, wheels squeaking over the floor, somebody talking on the corridor telephone. Once somebody got so flustered that an instrument tray went down with a loud clatter. Sssh came a voice, well above a whisper. You'll wake the dead.

Through the walls. They close me in, standing at right angles. What comes through is too much, being so little, hints only and as such unbearable. My imagination gets to work and makes it worse, perhaps.

I can look through the window. Mostly I look at it, trying to measure it up, decide whether it is a square, always failing to come to a conclusion. But when I forget about this nagging problem which is, after all, irrelevant, I am able to look through the window. But then the branch cuts across and obscures my vision. The old man's arm would claw at me if it could. If I could only get at it I would hack it off, but if I were able to reach it I would not want to, because then I would see the whole tree, and what lay beyond it. If it were possible, if one could see it, the thick ribbed trunk, branches stretching in all directions, held in mid-air, a suspended explosion, roots reaching far down into rich brown earth, if one could see it move to fill out the space available for its growth, thick buds breaking, then one would marvel, the heart would be flooded, limbs would prickle with new life, eyes bathed in grateful tears.

If. But the walls are in the way. Everything has turned to stone. The branch is amputated, dead.

I sigh, heavily. I am about to shift in the bed to ease my buttocks, perhaps lift myself on my elbows, when I remember: I cannot. I will not be able to move.

4

Voices outside, beyond the door. One loud and harsh, the other softer. Both men. I know them, and go rigid.

The door opens, but only slightly, towards the window where I cannot see. A long pause: I hold my breath. Yes, well, it's very curious. What's her ESR? Mm. Very odd. I've got a suspicion this may turn out to be something for Johnson, but we'll have to wait and see.

The door opens wider, they stroll in, both of them.

I look to the young man for reassurance. He usually has a sympathetic manner, but today he is in collusion with his friend, the senior man. I try to catch his eye but he is consulting his notes and speaking in diffident tones to the consultant, a showy man with grey hair and a loud voice. He seems convinced of his own cleverness, and spends his time trying to convince other people of it. That is what the patients are here for, helpless, in no position to deny him.

Well, well, well, and how are we this morning?

He looks at me, scratching the side of his nose. Up till now he has been playing with coins of small change in his pocket.

You're a bit of a puzzle, you know. We can't find anything wrong with you.

Something must be.

Oh, I agree.

They seem to regard this as a joke. Both are smiling, glancing at each other. The young doctor has a soft face.

Is something worrying you?

No.

Sure?

Not that I can think of . . . well, obviously, you'd be worried if you couldn't walk.

He hesitated for a moment, as though the possibility of putting himself in my position had not occurred to him before. He turned away, looked over his shoulder and said:

We're doing what we can.

After that he turned back conspiratorially to the registrar so that both backs were in my direction. They moved towards the window, shoulders almost touching, talking in subdued voices. The young doctor nodded, wrote something down. He was slightly taller than the older man, who was altogether denser, with lined and grainy skin. The hairs on his head varied from black to white, giving an overall effect of metallic grey. I could not hear the words, only sounds, as the two profiles moved against the window.

The older man, hands in trouser pockets, white coat open to display a natty suit, suddenly swung round and came towards the bed.

Um . . . I'd like to have a word with your husband. Would you ask him to come and see me on his next visit?

I lowered my eyelids so as to avoid looking into his face. I was a small and cunning animal now, hiding.

I had said nothing, not a word.

Would you do that? Or should I get in touch with him?

I shook my head.

No, I said at last, with difficulty. Please don't. He won't be coming. And it has nothing to do with him.

Well, who can I talk to? Who is coming to see you?

I don't know. My daughter, she's coming. But I don't want her bothered. She's much too young, anyhow.

How old is she?

Sixteen.

He scratched the side of his nose again, watching me, considering.

I must talk to somebody. For your sake. You do understand, don't you?

I think so.

I said it slowly. I was still suspicious. Why did he not speak to me, directly?

Is there a close friend, or perhaps a sister, who comes to see you?

I don't have anybody like that. Only a brother. He came once. Stood there fiddling with his hat brim. But you wouldn't get anything from talking to him. He doesn't understand, about anything. Never did. He was always too young when it mattered, and now . . . I don't think he'll come in again.

I've already had a chat with your brother. He came to see me. He was very worried about you. I lay silent. So that was it. The doctor had been talking to him, that accounted for it. What had they been saying? I recalled his embarrassed manner, his nervous haste, fiddling with his hat brim and glancing at his watch till he could decently leave.

The grey-haired, eminent consultant leaned over and patted my wrist with his left hand. He wore a gold ring on the fourth finger.

Well, we must just do our best, mustn't we?

I was sorry, now he was moving towards the door with his back to me, because I was suddenly prepared to like him. It had been an unexpected, fatherly gesture. I hoped he would turn at the door and say good-bye, but he did not. The young doctor opened the door for him and he passed through. I had already ceased to exist. But just before closing the door behind him the young man with his head of black hair turned round and smiled at me.

I'll come and see you later, he said.

5

I feel uncomfortable now. I preferred it before, just lying here, expecting nothing. Now I am tight as a strung bow. Since he has promised to come back I lie with my body tense and my face turned towards the door. I am also listening intently for sounds in the corridor. I am not sure how to act with regard to him, considering the difference in our ages. Also the degree to which his behaviour is professional is unknown. He appears to go out of his way to be charming to me, and since he is young and very good-looking I do not know how to respond. He puts his hands on my limbs, runs his fingers down my flesh, and this reminds me of other things, which is embarrassing. I look down to avoid looking into his face. I lose my bearings when it is him because I do not know how he regards me, or what I am meant to read into his frequent smiles. With a much older man there is no problem, his grey hairs and authority protects us both, so that the proper distance is kept. Like a father, it is good that he should keep slightly aloof, even if it hurts, even if I hate him as a result.

I am permitted to think him not human, the consultant, since he claims to be something more. I allow him to go on thinking how superior he is, knowing in my heart that he is less than nothing. Dirt.

But the young registrar, that is another matter.

I am thrown by his diffident manner, his alarming youth, the gentleness of his hands.

Also, he is liable to appear in my room unexpectedly, at curious times. Once he came in very late at night, it was already dark, the day staff had gone off duty, only the shaded lamp above my bed was switched on, giving a feeling of intimacy. We discussed philosophy. I do not know why he came, perhaps he himself forgot, but he sat on the edge of my bed and told me of a book he had read. That started it. He had not been able to get it out of his mind; obviously it had made a great impression on him.

I forgot that I was sick, and that he was my doctor.

At other times I am only too aware of my position. He asks me personal questions, looking into my face. His eyes are soft and dark. Impossible to distinguish their colour, but a harsh word like black does not fit. Then I speculate about his motives, his background and personal life, because I know he is really listening for the answer. He holds his head poised, slightly to one side, and I know he is waiting for the answer because he has almost stopped breathing. Only what does he make of me, of the things I tell him?

He examines my body, and I am not supposed to feel such shame of the way it looks. It is there, between us, the object of our study and concern. If I feel nothing, even the scratch of his car key on the soles of my feet, tears prickle in my eyes. I wish I could respond. But I feel nothing. The simplest reflex does not appear to work. But I do feel his hands on the surface of my body.

I speak to him. It does not occur to me to tell him lies.

Superficially he is interested in my family history. I avoided telling him about my father, or perhaps the subject did not come up.

He asked about diseases, deaths in the family. I told him about my grandmother, how it was the first death I could remember, though I never saw her dying. I did not go to the hospital, or the funeral. How it hit my mother, hard; I remembered thinking, how odd, since they used to bicker day after day. But he did not want to hear any of this. What did she die of?

She had a fall, fractured something. Her hip, I think it was.

Anyhow, I didn't think about it much at first, because I was young and things like that did not seem very serious. Although I knew, because my mother told me, that old people's bones often take a long time to mend. It might even, she said, never heal at all. She wore herself out going to the hospital. She shouldn't have done it, because she'd only just come back after a major operation. It meant standing around, waiting for buses, out till all hours in the streets, since there was nobody else to cope, nobody with a car, that is, till one day she came back and just sat there with her coat still on, exhausted, staring into space, and announced: she's dying. As though she could not believe it. She'd been having stomach trouble for months beforehand, and it was that, not the fall, they had operated to put a pin in, but she had stomach cancer all along.

Diseases run in families, which is why he is asking questions about the past.

At the moment, he said, putting his hand on mine, we don't regard such things as hereditary.

I stared at the wall, conscious of his watching me.

Everything recurs, I said. I have a feeling. It follows.

We have absolutely no conclusive medical evidence. Put it out of your mind, he said, patting my hand.

I turned to look at him.

It's my mother I'm worried about.

He nodded: I understand that, and I'm sure we're doing all we can for her. You're not to worry.

I visualized her lying in bed, nobody coming to visit her. She would be puzzled, and easily distressed.

I'd be grateful, I said, if you'd drop in to see her during the day. Just now and then, if you can spare a moment.

I'll do all I can: now you're not to fret.

You see, she's got nobody other than me. My father . . .

I stopped.

Now you're not to worry, he said. And I want you to promise me that you will eat properly. You're getting very thin, hardly more than a bag of skin and bone.

I told him I had lost all interest in food. Sometimes I could not bear to swallow the stuff.

We must try and do something about that, he said before leaving.

6

I can hear the lunch trolley outside the door. Meals always come at a peculiarly early hour in this place. Like being back in childhood.

I doubt whether I can swallow anything.

In the corridor the sound of voices used to be almost deafening. Pupils queueing for the second shift, whilst the lower school came out through the doors. By the time the second shift came into the hall bits of mashed potato and the odd processed pea lay spattered under the rows of tables and benches, to be kicked round the dusty floor. The smell of food took one's appetite away, and the process was completed by the sight of the line of servers, middle-aged females ladling food from vast bins. Then as now, the sound of metal spoons banging dollops of food on to cheap white plates. It was not permissible to refuse, walk down the line with an empty plate which one then left, so it did not much matter what you chose, you might as well accept everything. But there were punishments for pupils who left uneaten food on their plates, so one waited for a chance to slip out of the hall when the teacher's back was turned. I was caught once, given a detention for leaving a plateful of food, but I told the teacher I could not stay behind after school because I had to see my mother. He was very tall. I had to look up at him. I fingered the doorkey hanging on a string round my neck, saw him looking at it. He had greying sideburns: a man about my father's age. My father was always out, I told him, there was nobody to look after my younger brother. I would have to prepare his supper. Yes, all right, he said, you can go. I was ready to tell him everything. About the clean nightgown I would wrap up in a paper parcel for her, about waiting at the bus stop in the dark, how cold it was. Yes, all right, he repeated: I said you could go.

At any moment now the lunch tray will be brought in. Lack of exercise takes one's appetite away, it stands to reason. An invalid cannot be forced to eat.

Supercilious bastard. I could have told him a thing or two.

The orderly has come in. She now slides a tray on to the locker. She reminds me of the worn-out women who used to work in the school kitchen. For talking in class or unnecessary impudence we were sent down to the kitchen to scrub bowlfuls of potatoes in cold water, scoop out eyes with the point of a knife. I was fastidious at that age, loathed the skin of my hands smelling of raw potatoes and damp dishcloths, but they took it for granted, gossiping as they shifted huge boilers in their overalls. It was a good job, started mid-morning after they had cleared up the house and finished early enough for them to get home and prepare tea and supper for the family.

Can you manage now, dearie?

The door has closed. I am alone again. The food looks cold already. I can see no wavering vapour, signifying warmth. Soon it will become stone cold, the surface congealed. Like the room. My eye travels from the plate to the walls, examining the silence between them. My mother used to say: I haven't enjoyed a meal in years. The trouble with food is having to cook it yourself. By the time it is ready a woman has no appetite. But nobody could keep her out of the kitchen.

Eating out she considered a wicked waste of money, whilst tins and packaged stuff were no substitute for the real thing, downright unhealthy. After I moved in with the baby she spent hours sieving food, grating apples, mashing stuff. It was almost as though she belonged there, had come back to her true element. I dared not question how much was really necessary. It would have been like questioning her right to exist.

When I first started working, I remember, I used to enjoy going out for lunch during my hour off. On what I earned I had to eat very cheaply. Everywhere was crowded out. You had to fight your way through the door, it was such a crush, look all round for a seat. But I liked that, at first.

The fly has come back. It is walking round the edge of my plate, probing into the mashed potato. A first-year nurse has popped her head round the door: I've been told to come and see you eat your lunch. She was smiling happily. She sat on the edge of my bed and propelled a fork loaded with potato in the direction of my face. It was cold, and clung to my tongue, teeth, and the walls of my mouth. Finally I swallowed most of it. Who told you? I asked. She was preparing another forkful, this time meat and vegetables were included. Staff nurse. I expect the doctor talked to her. Can't have you losing weight. The forkful was poised, waiting in mid-air. If I could keep talking . . . It's cold, I said, looking plaintively at her. Well, who's fault is that? Come on now, be a good girl.

She fed me, mouthful by mouthful. I drew it out as long as I could. It became almost a game, one I had played as a child. You eat mouthfuls, not for yourself, but for the sake of those who love you: one for mummy, daddy, granny, going through all those to whom you belong. The whole web of relationships is driven home with unappetizing food. Reluctant, you become willing.

54

She even wiped my chin for me after a gobbet of food went astray.

There now, she said, that wasn't so bad, was it? She got up, put the fork back on to the empty, smeared plate.

It reminded me of school dinners, I said. Did you have them?

Ugh, she said.

Suddenly we were the same age. She laughed. Comradely: girls together. Then she picked up the tray and left the room.

7

I must have dozed a little. My body is lead, it sinks through the surface on which I am supposedly lying. I am lying in it, somehow, as in water. Once or twice I have been conscious of nurses coming in. The glass tube of a thermometer was stuck through my lips. A sound of paper wrapping, unwrapped, crumpled up.

I must have dozed a little, but I cannot remember dreaming. Only that the walls have become indistinct. Whiter. The window opposite my bed has become larger. I can see outside, the whole tree. And the garden in which it stands. Small, of course, rather bare, enclosed by the building itself on three sides. I should have known. I have seen it before: it looks so familiar.

Freedom, how the mind can float: I had forgotten it. Standing at the base of the tree, feet getting damp, one hand on the rough bark, looking up into the branches, studying how they fork off from each other to make a pattern against the sky. Like blood vessels in the brain: it feeds, and functions. Horse chestnut, perhaps, or elm, who knows, I'm not much good at nature. Impossible to say now, during winter, whilst it has no foliage. But afterwards comes spring, the buds will suddenly break, so fast, the eruption takes your breath away. There was a smell of soot in the air, gritty, almost pungent, but it was preferable to the smell inside, one she now associated with that particular hospital and would later think of in connection with all hospitals. Some sort of disinfectant, no doubt. A dog had got in somehow, perhaps through the railings, it meandered in a zigzag, as though searching for something, pissed against the iron foot of the bench, and vanished into the bushes. She (that is, I) ran her, that was my fingers down the ridges of bark, feeling the crusted growth. My eye then travelled up to study the geometry of the branches. I found that soothing, somehow, I realized with an interest that amounted to pleasure that thousands of leaves would be arranged, layer upon layer, to get maximum light, with scientific logic and artistic skill. At least, I think that was what I thought. It was a long time ago. I may be adding things, insights I became conscious of much later. She was still very young then, rather graceful and slender. I must have been a graceful figure, standing there, under the tree.

I stood under the tree, thinking . . . I don't know what I was thinking. Lost in thought, anyhow, when I felt his hand touch my elbow. I want to talk to you, he said.

You're taking it too hard, he said. Come and sit down on the bench. These things happen. She'll get over it. So, for that matter, will you.

I was too cold, standing under the tree, wearing only a thin dress. But I had rushed out without thinking. The dress was made of a filmy material, draped from the shoulder and pulled in at the waist.

You're shivering, he said, and put his arm round me. You're cold.

Look at me, he said. We had sat down on the bench. I stared at the fingers in my lap, twisting, interlocking. He lifted my chin with his hand and forced me to look him in the face. You've been crying, he said. I sniffed, my eyelids quickly lowered. I was twisting a damp handkerchief in my lap.

This is an odd sort of garden, I said, trying to sound natural. Do you sometimes come here?

Yes, he said. Sometimes, in the summer. It used to be a churchyard. Look, you can still see a few tombstones in the long grass, up against that wall. My eyes followed his finger. The old stone slabs looked pitted, perhaps with city grime, their inscriptions now illegible.

I laughed. How very appropriate. Nobody has far to go.
He smiled.
I want to be useful.

He said it so quietly, so seriously, that I was embarrassed at having made such a joke.

It must be marvellous, I said, being able to help people. I would like to do something like that. Only . . . Only I was squeamish, of bodies, and suffering. Nor did I have the application, even if I'd had the chance. A girl's place, certainly mine, was first and foremost in the house.

Now you're being romantic, he said. It's not so marvellous. Often I feel helpless.

Anyhow, he said, you'll do something useful. You're doing it now. And you'll be very important to somebody.

She stared at him. Her lip trembled. Important, she said, what do you mean? You know what I mean, he said.

At this point she must have broken the tension by talking about her mother. Impossible to know where such a conversation could otherwise have led. He was impressed by her concern, a sense of responsibility beyond her years. Tried to reassure her. I like your nose, he said. He was determined to make her laugh.

I felt his hand on my elbow. I felt an absurd desire to talk to

him about the tree near the bench. How I had thought about
it when he found me standing there, the way the sun would
catch translucent green cells in a pattern of ascending, spread-
ing planes. But he would have thought me mad, or at least
slightly crazy. So I said nothing.

He leaned back to rest his head on the bench and yawned. A
patient had died in the night: he had been called out of bed.
His throat looked very frail inside the shirt collar, visible
under his white coat. You see, he said, how the leaves seem to
go in an ascending pattern, so that the whole tree catches the
maximum light. It's rather marvellous, when you come to
think of it.

His stethoscope was dangling out of his pocket, between the
slats of the bench.
    Careful, I said, you'll lose your stethoscope.
    We both laughed. Our hands touched. He put his hand
over mine.

He spoke my name . . . I can't remember what it was . . . but
he spoke my name.

I began to shiver. Goose pimples on my arms. You've been
crying, he said, you mustn't do that. He saw drops sparkle in
my eyes. As in films, they sparkled visibly in the dark.
    I sniffed, embarrassed. No I haven't, I said. Crying always
made my nose look unsightly.

This is ridiculous.

We talked sanely and sensibly about my mother's condition.
He told me I must not overdo things. Convalescents could be
very demanding and difficult, a sure sign that their health was
improving. Once they started getting better they became per-
nickety about small things, always fussing about trifles which

they would not have cared about when they were really ill. I was not to allow myself to be run round in circles, I was doing more than enough as it was. Or I would be ill next, which would help nobody.

I can't become ill, I said.

He laughed. You're an obstinate young lady.

I was sitting up very straight, with my chin stuck out firmly.
But I admire you for it.

He took my chin in his large hand and shook it lightly, teasingly, the way one shakes a puppy who will not let go of a ball.

I must go back inside and talk to mother. And what about you, doctor? Won't they be searching the hospital for you?
I know. But before you go, there was something I wanted to say to you.
Yes?

It hung on the air, unanswered.
Yes?

A nurse had opened the double doors leading back into the building, now she stood on the step in the fading light, her white cap and starched apron showing clearly through the gloom. Doctor! He got up, began to run after he heard: Please, it's urgent.

He had an important job, I realized that, while I was only an ignorant schoolgirl. Sometimes distance and professional etiquette made demands which became intolerable for both of us. A necessary silence. I could see that the strain was beginning to tell on him. He was quite startled when we nearly collided at the angle where two corridors met. Come into the garden for a moment, he said. I want to talk to you.

What have you been doing? he asked. I shrugged, avoided looking at him. I felt a sort of leaden indifference: what does one do, or say?

He said something, but at that very moment the lights beyond the iron railings changed, traffic accelerated and the din drowned his words. What did you say? I shouted above the noise, but I am not sure he had heard even so much. Meanwhile, I could see he was waiting for an answer. Afterwards, when the moment had passed, I guessed what he had said, but it was too late to make the right reply. He was frowning, studying his finger-nails, then looked across at the rows of windows opposite. It would sound quite wrong now.

A little later he said to me, still speaking above the traffic noise: I am puzzled about your mother, something about her manner. She is not making as fast a recovery as she should. There is no medical reason. I nodded. I could imagine: All day she lies, watching the visitor's chair at the foot of her bed, waiting. She could, he says, get up now, and take a few steps, but she has no wish to. She has no appetite, scarcely touches her food, and often does not answer when someone speaks to her. She appears not to hear. I did not know where to start: he wanted an explanation, but it was too complex, one should keep up appearances, he was only a man, after all, like other men, sympathetic certainly, kind as no one else I had wanted to confide in, but whom, in the last analysis, could one really trust?

I know, I said.

He waited, but I said nothing.

It is such a long day, I said, finally. She imagines things. All day she lies watching that chair, waiting for someone to come and see her. I try to make it up to her, but the days are still too long.

It all weighed like a lead ball, what I was keeping from him.

I could feel it in my chest, expanding against my ribs. I wanted to trust him, I needed to. But he was also no doubt like my father, being a man, imponderable, mysterious. There was something about the breed I had not reckoned with till now.

You look tired, he said. You'll make yourself ill. I warned you.
I could not cope much longer, running the household going to school each day and trying to catch up on homework worried about everything. He ran one forefinger down the side of my face, very gently and slowly. I did not flinch. I could imagine how I looked, the dark shadows under my eyes.
The days are too short, I said, sighing.
He laughed. Just now you said they were too long.

I have an idea, he told me hurriedly, and outlined his plan. We discussed it. Almost without thinking he took hold of my hand, almost without thinking I allowed him to put his arms round me. Then I remembered: who I was, the circumstances in which we all lived. I shall have to consider, I told him, drawing back. There isn't much time he told me, I shall have to know by the end of this week. And we walked back inside to tell my mother. Except for her, it was almost decided.

The building was made of concrete, long and white, gleaming oddly in the half light of wintry days at the edge of the sea. Grey sky, grey water, both constantly in motion, and behind the stillness of darker land. The sound of the sea washed into the bedrooms, all of which faced outward, towards it, and at night visitors dozed off with the sound of waves drumming in their ears. During the day most of the patients lay stretched out in the sun lounge, wrapped up in rugs, watching the grey sky through the glass, and the water below churning over and over itself, getting nowhere, beating with futile pressure against rocks and retaining wall. Sometimes a pale sun shone in a break between clouds, and seawater rising in a high hopeless splurge sparkled, gleaming in sunlight for a moment before splattering back on to stonework like squashed insects, black and lifeless, to evaporate with the wind. I would walk a little, though watching the dark foaming mass gave me a feeling of vertigo, and the wind cut through my clothes. I walked bent, like a pocket knife. Meanwhile my mother spent most of her time in the sun lounge, staring at the sea, or upstairs in her room. Sometimes I would bring her meals up there, when she did not want to join the other patients in the communal dining room. She was getting stronger, but her wound had not healed properly and she was also being treated for anaemia. He came down regularly to monitor her progress, and I waited patiently for his arrival. Twice a week, I think it was. During the days between I sniffed the sea air, became conscious of the changing weather, went out for short walks, and swallowed dull but wholesome meals in the large communal dining room. Most of the other patients were elderly, but I did not mind having no one of my own age to talk to. If my mother did not come down I would sit by myself and observe people, how they moved forks slowly into their mouths with a slight turn of the head, masticated, engaged in desultory small talk. After lunch most of the patients would go to their rooms to sleep, after carefully pushing their chairs back against the long table, moving slowly towards the door of the dining room. I would go up too. Perhaps I would have to wait, because we had to be careful. Not to be seen together, not to be overheard. He would come to my room and make love, whispering in the small room. Every sound had to be muffled, subdued. The walls were thin. I think my mother had no inkling, neither of us told her anything, I did not so much as hint at the truth, and she was too wrapped up in her own concerns, her own body and the slow sensations of progress back to health, to become aware of what was happening to anybody else. But she must have noticed how solicitous he was, and perhaps she misunderstood his concern for her welfare. She remarked that he was such a good doctor. And another time he had apparently discussed something with her for over an hour, family life, I think it was, and told her about his own background. Or it might have been philosophy. I hope she was not misguided enough to think that his attention had anything to do with her.

He was, of course, a good doctor. Professionally he would leave nothing undone that could be done. Equally his concern for her health, and thus welfare, was genuine.

I dreaded the homecoming. I knew this could not go on for ever. When we arrived back at the empty house, those dusty and gloomy rooms, with the curtains drawn, she would have to face the truth.

So would I. It occurred to me that she was already coming to terms with it: that this explained her withdrawal and lack of concern for her surroundings or anybody else.

I visualized her sitting in the empty house over the years counting out the hours of her life like stitches on a knitting needle. We would be required, her son especially, to wear her labour as a sign of love. I wanted to do something, but if I tried the handiwork would become a tangled mess. She would

64

shed tears of rage and frustration. I would try, instead of grabbing the wool and chucking the whole lot in the dustbin, to console her: look, I said, it's all right, laboriously picking up the stitches and handing it back to her.

If only this limbo could last, for as long as necessary. Wind sweeping the coastline clean, the air curiously sharp and biting, wiping out thought. Rising grey cloud looks luminous. The day brightens. I am swept along by the wind like a detached leaf, having nowhere to go, and, being lost, find something of myself. I came back to the warm and stuffy rooms. Old ladies hovered, holding on to sticks. They hardly spoke.

I hardly spoke. I breathed in the fresh air, watched clouds changing shape and moving fast overhead. I noticed trees beginning to break out, green sprouting out of damp earth, the first sudden shower of blossom. But my mother was getting bored: she spoke of going home. I tried to dissuade her, but she was worried about my brother, who had been boarded out with the family of a schoolfriend. I'm well enough now, she said, and I want to see him. He misses his own home. So do I. I want my own things. I've got a job to do, can't go on lolling about like this. To say nothing of your father.

Say nothing of your father. Coward. So the truth had not been faced.

Just a few more days, I pleaded. Then we'll go home. A breathing space, blank. Like white paper: seen from the edge it is nothing, almost invisible. On the paper it is possible to write a story, fill up the surface.

I waited for his regular visit, but he did not come. He usually took the mid-morning train, always arrived at the same time. Something had gone wrong. I waited: two more days passed

E 65

without any sign from him. For the first time my body ached for his presence. I had not understood my luck before. On the third day I went to the matron and asked if she had heard anything. We were due to leave and my mother was naturally anxious. A brisk and kindly woman with greying hair, she looked at me for a long time without saying a word. I felt confused but held my ground. I'm afraid, she said, there has been an accident. I stood speechless at the door of her office. She was obviously not prepared to say more. Is it very bad? I asked finally, my voice scarcely above a whisper. I'm afraid so.

I went away. He would not be coming. It was none of my business, she had inferred, with her dismissal. But I was also afraid that it had been no accident. The word accident was a euphemism, it could be spoken, but there was a hint in her reticence of something more, indecent, awful. I tried to think what I had done to contribute to this dreadful gashed wound which had suddenly opened, the unthinkable pain. But I could think of nothing. I was left in the dark, quite alone.

You're very quiet, said my mother. She was holding up a wool dress, now she folded it in half across the suitcase lying on the bed, tucked in the sleeves. Aren't you glad to go home? I should have thought you would be bored in a place like this. I did not answer, kept my face to the window. Something was bleeding inside. If I had not been the cause, then I had nothing to do with any of it. I saw how the mass of water shattered on concrete and rock. It was flung into the air and splattered on to the surface of the esplanade, making dark marks. It tasted salt. I could taste it on my face.

Perhaps it was better to destroy him in the first flush of youth. The alternative was only a slow death. It had been a handsome face, regular features and dark hair, blanching now, it was fading fast as the life blood ran out of the gap. Soon I would forget it, I would not be able to recall how he had looked.

When I close my eyes I only recall the wound: it looks remarkably fresh and lifelike, as though the blood was still wet. I cannot recall the face.

8

I lie immobile. It could not happen now, so long as I am inactive. I feel sleepy and quite calm: only a few old scars which cannot give trouble.

I had a dream: I found myself attending a medical lecture. I was sitting high up, right at the back of a curved lecture hall in semi-darkness, looking down on a man speaking in an area brightly illuminated by overhead lights. He paced up and down the wooden platform as he spoke, occasionally indicating the blackboard behind him, and I had no idea of the gist of what he was saying. I must have come in after the lecture started. I was studying the backs of heads and shoulders below me, all I could see of the bodies below me. The old-fashioned rows of seats had high backs, one sat boxed in. But my attention had been held by a man's narrow head, the shape and dark hair looked familiar, I was sure it was him, if only, if only he would turn round for a moment so I could see his face. I willed him to, beaming my longing into his impenetrable skull, trying to make my presence palpable. But, oblivious, somewhere in the past, he did not move. Nothing would make him turn his head, nor was it possible to make a noise, interrupt and thus draw attention to oneself. I was also conscious that I had no place in this awesome professional circle, I had sneaked in and now did not understand what was going on. His head, rows of heads, were all listening attentively to the spate of learning coming from the platform. The speaker now stopped pacing, gripped the lectern with both hands, and looked round his audience, as though studying them. Give me, he said after a pause, a definition of death. Half his face was in shadow, only his nose and cheekbones still caught the light. Voices came from the auditorium: no breathing, circulation, cessation of brain activity. I saw how the skin stretched taut across his forehead, gleaming with hair loss. He listened, patronizingly polite, until it was time to give his answer. A patient is dead when the wound stops bleeding.

The voice in my head. I woke with tears running down my face. I do not know why, but perhaps it was gratitude. Everything was clear now.

My arm is numb because I have been lying on it. I release it and the blood begins to tingle in the limb. It is necessary, but gradually the returning circulation feels unpleasant, then painful. I can only wait for it to pass.

I lie with my eyes half closed, seeing nothing through my eyelashes. Somebody has touched my hand. A nurse was standing beside my bed, holding a bulk of white paper. Wrapped round something. Somebody has sent you flowers, she said. Aren't you a lucky girl. I'll put them in water for you.

9

He was standing beside my bed. I opened my eyes and saw his face, his dark eyes studying me. I did not know how long he had been waiting for me to come back to consciousness. Or if he had just disturbed me. He smiled.

You've been asleep.

I was far from sure, confused. I did not know whether this consciousness now was dreaming or if the sequence which had previously troubled me had been simply a figment of mind. Nor did I know how I was meant to occupy my body, whether, and if so, how, these limbs joined on to each other, and what I should be required to think in order to make it function.

I had not yet recalled that this body was not now expected to work.

I smiled back. Warm, sleepily. Not since childhood had there been such a drama of sleeping and being woken, watched. Cradled on stories.

How odd. I suppose I must have been.

His hand took hold of the top edge of the bedclothes. He was about to pull them back.

Now then, let's have a look at you.

The rubber tube of the stethoscope was snaking across the bed cover as he leaned towards me. Any moment now my warm cocoon, fuzzy at the edges, would be destroyed.

His dark, narrow head moved sideways, distracted by something unusual. A mass of flowers stood arranged on the locker, occupying the empty space.

My, he said, what beautiful flowers.

The weight lifted. I had forgotten that the temperature in this white and even room was also carefully regulated: there was no difference between the air above and below the cover which had been removed from me. I turned my head to avoid his immediate scrutiny and saw the gift which stood near my head. The roses had dark red heads, a colour which reminded me of wounds, so deep, so tender the fleshy texture. The bruised purplish petals folding in on themselves, but perhaps they would soon open up in the warm room, their cut stalks visible in the water, through the glass. Each head on a long stalk, conspicuous thorns running down its rigid length.

Very defensive things, roses. But soon will come the betrayal. The tight head will open, reveal all, and bleed to death.

He pulled up my nightgown. The skin of my abdomen shrank. Who sent them to you? They look terribly expensive.

And therefore guilty. An attempt at atonement, riddled with unspoken guilt.

I don't know. I was asleep when the nurse brought them in.

Are my hands so cold? Try to relax.

The colour is the same as the stuff they took out of my arm this morning. They look like wounds, don't they doctor, absolutely heavy with blood? Soon they will begin to drip.

There's no need to be morbid. Nobody is planning to cut you open. They look very nice to me. Now, I'm going to touch you in various places and I want you to tell me whether you have any sensation. Don't watch me, just say.

Perhaps you could cut me open.

He looked startled, stopped in mid-air.

Would you like that?

I shook my head, conscious of a serious slip, the gulf beneath our feet widening with each second.

Of course not. But I had a dream, just before you arrived. You were in the dream, as a matter of fact.

The narrow crack was gradually growing into an abyss of uncertainties. I could not step across.

And?

71

Somebody told me that bleeding is a sign of life.

Up to a point.

So perhaps you should cut me to find out whether I am alive or dead.

That seems a bit drastic. You do have curious dreams, I must say. Surely you don't want to get hurt?

Yes . . . No . . . I don't know. Pain is a sign of life, isn't it?

I suppose so. It's an odd way of putting it.

He continued to examine me.

Can you feel this?

His hands moved gently, almost lovingly, with carefully trimmed nails.

No.

And this?

I shook my head.

Now I want you to close your eyes. Did you feel anything?

Yes.

And now.

Yes.

Good. That's marvellous. You didn't yesterday.

He had covered me up again. I lay there, waiting. He was writing down notes in my file, not looking at me. He suddenly looked up, took a quick breath.

I think we're getting somewhere. He stared at the blank wall, then looked sideways at me. He was perched on the edge of the bed. Do you often have such morbid thoughts?

I shrugged, No, not really. I suppose it's my position.

What position?

This.

I gestured with my hand at the prone body running down from my head to my feet, the shape of a log under the cover.

What do you think is wrong with you?

I hadn't thought about it, not really, I mean that's your job, isn't it, and I don't see what it's got to do with me. I try not to worry about things, I mean there's no point in that, on the other hand I've had a hard life and there is no use in not looking facts in the face.

What facts?

I withdrew my eyes from his face and thought about my ravaged face, slack breasts, somebody had sucked them dry, the flesh beginning to curdle like soured milk both at the top of my thighs and elsewhere, nothing could contain its shape, it bulged out of elastic garments, the tired skin flopped. I looked down towards my impotent legs and, feeling embarrassed, hoped he would misunderstand my silence.

As a child, I said finally, I was frightened of being buried alive, because I could not conceive of being dead. Now I feel already half-dead. Not literally, because of my lower half, I used to feel it before. As though one is being reduced the whole time, until there is nothing left, and death is simply the logical termination.

But you're not going to die.

I laughed. A nervous, hollow laugh. He was being remarkably obtuse, this young man, or he must think me very stupid.

We think there is nothing wrong with you. All our tests suggest that your body is perfectly normal.

This was an unexpected shock. There was a silence, while he waited for me to react.

Are you sure?

As sure as one can be of anything.

I considered this new situation. Until now I had felt myself in harmony with my surroundings, convinced of the logic of this room in which I found myself lying. Now I was called upon to defend my helpless position.

I suppose it all depends on the angle from which you are looking, I said. After all, there must be something wrong with me—or I wouldn't be here. I was almost proud of my irrefutable argument. Unless, of course, everything else is wrong.

Leaving myself out of it. I had removed myself, bundled up the world with him in it, and tossed it away.

I had expected him to be annoyed or offended, instead he

continued to sit on the edge of my bed, thinking, to judge by his expression. For the first time I felt that he was not about to rush off, mentally already attending to his next patient.

The word walking, he brought out, probing now, does it have any particular significance for you?

I giggled.

Oh doctor, we are becoming serious.

He did not react, but simply waited. I realized that at this juncture even joking would not work, was liable to be considered seriously.

My mother, who is now an elderly woman, fell down yesterday.

You were here before yesterday.

But I knew what would happen. Just as I already know how it will end. You can't lie to me.

What makes you say that? We haven't had the X-rays yet.

My mother's mother had a fall. Similar. That was a long time ago. A day, a number of days before now.

So, how will it end then?

You know too.

I told you: we are waiting for the results of the X-ray. As soon as I hear I will let you know.

I already know. What has happened must happen.

But the fact that the two accidents are similar is merely an unfortunate coincidence.

No. Not an accident. Not coincidental. I know what the X-rays will show, just as you know. I know what you will say, that at her advanced age healing is a long business, and we must not expect miracles. And all the time you will be lying about death. That what must come is inevitable. Every step is fraught with danger. One slip, one miscalculation is enough. A child knows this, it steps over the lines between paving stones, thinking to avoid evil. Afterwards we try to forget it, the unavoidable evil, because only a child believes in magic. There is only one solution: to stop. Since each step is a step in the same direction.

74

Which is?

You see, there can be only one direction. Do you know what I am talking about? (He was not taking any notes, but I was determined now, to make myself understood.) Walking through the fourth dimension. We all do it. Although it is invisible it is really the only one that exists. And it is also sinister. For the most part we do not realize where we are going, but it leaves marks on your face, etches lines, sucks in hollows, sows the seeds of a slow internal putrefaction. One day a blackbird leaves clawmarks round your eyes, nothing else marks its passage, but it will come back later to pick them out of your skull. The slope is so gradual you hardly notice that you are stepping downwards, until one day you find yourself a bag of bones, about to be tipped into the pit.

We remained still for a while, without moving or speaking. I heard his breathing and my own heartbeat within the four blank walls. I had envied his handsome head of dark hair, the smooth unmarked face.

You, too, I said.

Our silence had continued for a long time. He said nothing, sitting slackly on the edge of the bed. He seemed to be deep in thought. Then he raised his right arm and slowly touched the folded centre of a rose which stood with its head towards him, touched it lightly with the tip of one finger. His arm dropped again. I felt sorry for him, felt that I had somehow been unkind. I should not have unleashed so much. It almost amounted to aggression, since it was more than anybody could bear.

I'm sorry.

He said nothing.

I suppose you think I'm mad.

No.

Or bad. A malingerer of some sort.

He looked at me. I don't. The question is, which do you think?

75

I turned away and looked at the roses standing in the glass vase. I looked at the rose which I thought he had touched just now and tried to see a difference, but it looked undamaged.

I don't usually think about myself. I never have. I was taught never to, in fact if anything I was led to believe that it was bad to think of oneself at all. It was other people that mattered, certainly that's been the way in my life. I've always had to take charge, and I couldn't afford to lose control.

Sometimes one cannot afford not to lose control.

I know that. I think I realized that some some time ago.

He looked at me, straight in the eyes, and leaned forward.

Do you realize what you have just said?

I was bewildered, I thought it was the nearness of his body as he leaned forward, his dark gaze, but I could feel warmth, an uneasy tingling sensation in my chest which spread upward and which was much worse. Soon my throat was hot, my face burned, and I could feel tears prickling in my eyes. They overflowed. Felt cool as they dried. I put my hands over my face. The water ran down my face and between my fingers. My whole body shook.

10

It is nice lying here. It is warm. I am being fed, I am being washed. The nurses are kind.

I like the way everything is distant. The sound of traffic far away, muted. Soon it will start to get heavier, as everyone tries to get home. The street lights will go on, ignored at first, but the sky above will darken fast. The queue of office employees at the bus stop will grow to panic proportions, while the eyes of vehicles glare in the dark, unable to move forward. I lie here, happy in the knowledge that I do not have to move, wait for a bus with the number of my destination.

The struggle to get back was bad enough, but the moment of arrival was the worst. That awful house, dark and cold, with its empty spaces. Picking up circulars from the mat, switching on lights. Somebody might, I thought, have washed up, regarding the mess in the kitchen. I fumbled in my shopping bag, under the evening paper, for our supper: three chops.

The room is beginning to grow darker. Soon someone will put a hand round the door and switch on the centre light, a gentle moon, always conveniently at the full. Clouds do not penetrate these four white walls. I do not have to think: what shall I wear? should I take an umbrella? conscious that my shoes pinch, make my feet ache, after only two hours.

So far nobody has come, they seem to have forgotten, but I

do not mind. I like lying here while it grows darker, it is almost dark, the shadows creeping up on me. Outside the old man's arm is getting misty, the outline dimmed and now lost in the dusk. I hope it will break out into leaf one day. I hope so. I should like to think so.

A leaf, seen against the sun, is a webbed hand. The whole forest is a pattern of webbed hands, praying to the summer light.

The green cells which shone so translucent are burned dry. The hands shrivel and fall, are trodden into the mud.

Soon the tight buds become visible. It is a hope which aches to explode. It cannot be stopped, not without destroying the whole universe and the slightest germ of life.

I dreamed about putting the house up for sale and making a fresh start in new surroundings. Although I thought about it, finding a way of doing it was quite another matter. When I broached the subject she refused pointblank. I suppose it's not good enough for you, she said. No, I insisted, conscious of my indebtedness, finding it impossible to give the real reason. Which would have been misunderstood as ingratitude of the most hurtful kind.

And anyhow, she said, after I had tried unsuccessfully to drop the subject, what would I do, cooped up in a flat all day? Forget it, mother, I said, but she would not. She began reminding me of my grandmother, what the bombing had done to her. Losing her home had done something to her, it was not just the shock, no, though that was bad enough. As though the incendiary had taken her insides out, her very guts, it was not just bricks and mortar but her pride that was shattered, something that went on till her dying day.

No need to remind me. I heard about it often enough.

Escape was, therefore, not possible. The house was dark; each door, each piece of stained woodwork, was impregnated with pain. It came out and hit me when I looked, though what I thought I saw was dust, flaws where the wood splintered and caught at threads of clothing, a damp patch where the flocked wallpaper was beginning to come away. The child made marks on the wall which she tried to rub off with a damp cloth. Sometimes it worked, sometimes the mark stayed. I thought about stripping the walls, throwing out the old furniture, and bringing about a transformation. But she was satisfied with the place as it had always been, and the merest hint of change offended her. She bridled at the apparent assault, not only on her habits, but her good taste, a lifelong choice. You could always go, she said tartly, but made it clear how foolish, not to say selfish, such a move would be, not for her sake, but for the child's. And it was true that a child needed a garden to play in, space, that she seemed to thrive under my mother's daily care. This, I knew, I could not afford to replace elsewhere.

I like the functional modernity of this room. No unnecessary trappings, nothing personal. A replica, no doubt, of a thousand other rooms. The walls are smooth: nothing to grasp, hold on to.

I did once look at a flat which I saw advertised. Two small rooms, both about the size of this one, in a new building. But I did not see how I could make ends meet. Though she was at school by then there was the problem of holidays, and who would collect her, look after her before I got home at night? Suppose she got sick? You've got your own life to lead, he had said, though what business is it of his, I should like to know, she retorted, and I suppose she was right: he just did not like having my mother in the house when he brought me home, it embarrassed him, and she made no secret of her disapproval. We had an argument about him once, just before it finished. I should have thought you would have had more sense by now, she told me. I notice he hasn't offered to take any of the responsibility. How would you manage, pay for everything? Has he asked you to marry him? Well, has he?

I suppose I could not have left her anyhow. He was quite wrong about it: I have never had my own life to lead. It has always belonged to other people.

She had a boxful of objects, my grandmother, a few things which she had somehow managed to rescue from the rubble. She stored the box under her bed, and sometimes she would pull it out and show me what was inside. I was her only willing audience, although I had no recollection of the house which had been destroyed. With just a few knick-knacks, two chipped china ornaments, a metal toast rack, three apostle spoons, she reconstructed it. She showed me the shard of a dinner plate, ornamented in red and gold, to illustrate what her best dinner service, given to her as a wedding present, had been like. She used to wash them ever so carefully so nothing got broken, nobody else was allowed to handle them. They were ranged along a welsh dresser. There were hooks for the cups to hang by the handle. When the raids started they used to swing and rattle. She was frightened and took them down, stored them in a box. But she never managed to find it. She could not understand it, the war, why people had to do such terrible things. Sometimes she used to cry a little, about the past. Her gnarled hands with the creased skin stroked each thing, laid them carefully back. Her fingers were twisted with arthritis, the knuckles swollen like tree joints.

Mother called it junk. She tossed the whole lot out after her death. I would like to have kept something as a souvenir, but she tipped everything into the dustbin in a kind of fury. What was not broken before must now have been smashed or damaged, a cloud of dust rose from the previous detritus of ash and vegetable peelings. I doubt whether it would have been possible to find something small and unbroken like the apostle spoons. I also felt that if I tried to pick them out my mother's fury would turn on me. I don't think I had ever seen so much pent-up rage coming out of her. I was sorry: the things had reminded me of my childhood.

She could get angry, though not about the real things. I never heard her mention my father. I once saw her stamp a piece of charred toast into the kitchen floor, her face twisted. I was frightened, unsure. Well don't gawp, girl, she said, seeing me standing there, and bent down to pick up the bits. Go and fetch a dustpan and brush. And tell your brother to get on with his homework. She had plans for him, ambitions for his future, but he was easy-going and disinclined to take study seriously. Your headmaster says you could do better, so why don't you? How many times do I have to drum it into you? I told her about my own plans, since I was older: the art mistress said I was talented, I could get a place and study design. She looked at me, incredulous and bewildered, picked up the word "design" as though it were a soiled dishrag which had not been put back where it belonged. What kind of a job is that? Who is going to pay *you* to design something? Really, she said, I'm surprised at you, I thought you had more common sense, a practical head on your shoulders. I tried to argue, but I was timid, my vision evaporated like a silly dream. Which it no doubt was. Later she put my name down for a secretarial course. You know where you are, she said. Somebody has been putting silly ideas in your head, kindly, wishing to console me, it wasn't my fault, that's what comes of modern education, I'd like to give some of the teachers in your school a piece of my mind. Putting fancy ideas into girls' heads. No sense of reality. I suppose she told you that you were some kind of genius? Whatever happens, she said, you'll always be able to make a living if you've got shorthand and typing. And you may need it, she warned darkly, in one of the few, if indirect references to our own situation. Marriage isn't always what it's cracked up to be.

I remembered that remark, later. I don't understand you, she said on the day I came back to the house with my baby. Do you want the moon?

11

The nurse has come in. Why are you lying in the dark, she asks. You should have rung. She presses the switch near the door and the light flickers unsteadily for a moment before providing a steady illumination. I blink, but do not speak. The gleaming window is now a black square on white; everything has been reversed, the negative of photographic memory. The light is almost blinding: I can only guess at the old man's arm outside in the cold, a leafless branch in the dark. Beyond the pane of my fishtank. What would you like for tea? So soon, tea time has come round again. There's strawberry jam, she says, tucking in the bedclothes on my right, and scones. I'll bring you a scone.

She has left the room. Before going she remarked: what beautiful roses. I suppose they came from your husband? I should have asked the nurse if there was a card, when she discarded the wrapping. Now I shall never know. I can think of nobody who might have sent them.

I smiled, which she could accept as an answer. It made me feel safe, for a few moments, that she could assume his figure in the background. The curious word: husband. She assumes him as she has always assumed her own, lurking in shadows. Waiting for her. Lying in bed, cut off from the outside world, I can pretend. You are a lucky girl, she said. I smiled.

You don't know when you are well off, she argued, resting

her right hand on the teapot. She was always cold, her bluish-white hands had bony fingers and veins which bulged on the backs. Whenever she served tea she rested her hand on the pot so that the warmth would comfort her. She described him as quiet and thoroughly dependable, and we both knew why she found this an admirable quality. You'd be a fool, she said.

The chair is upholstered in a patterned material, two shades of brown. It stands waiting in the corner, quietly, with its back to the wall, under the window, behind the washbasin with its dripping tap.

You'd be a fool, she said, he's devoted to you, and you won't get a second chance like that. I could not put my finger on it, describe my doubt. I did not know what I wanted. You get on with him all right, don't you? I've never known you to quarrel. We had never quarrelled. I tried to pick a quarrel. Perhaps if we shouted and screamed at each other I would know, one way or the other. You can't treat a man like that, she warned me, he won't wait for ever, and panic seized me as I realized that I would never know. Any decision would be arbitrary and therefore wrong.

The chair has a supportive back, with curved wooden arms. It waits. The arms wait. Because the arms are joined at top and bottom they are helpless. Having no hands they are unable to grasp, and cannot hold.

You must admit, she said, he is thoughtful. Such beautiful flowers. You are a lucky girl. I wish I had a husband like that.

The chair waits, patiently. Not long to go now. It is almost the end of the day. You should have rung, she said. Why didn't you ring the bell? She thought it absurd of me to lie in the dark. I could have used the bulbous bellpush which is always tucked under my pillow. So far I have never used it. What could one legitimately ask for?

To me the roses are wounds, heavy with blood. They have thorns to make each other bleed.

I hoped for a terrible accident, to make things bleed, something which would take the decision out of my hands. I wanted to feel something, spontaneously, if only excruciating agony. Nothing happened. Things went on as before, only underneath the tension was building up, daily. I decided not to see him any more. He did not understand, but concurred. He always concurred with what he absurdly regarded as my wishes. More days went by. I made a fetish of being always punctual, always punctilious and conscientious at the office, but it was useless, a shorthand typist is not required to be anything more, and nobody even noticed. After a few days I was so fed up with myself and my surroundings that I could have stepped under a bus. I thought about it in the lunch hour. Everything was the same for five days of the working week, and nothing at the weekend to look forward to. Nothing unexpected happened. I did not meet anyone. Nobody spoke to me, or even wrote. I hoped that the man who was sharing my table in the snack bar would say something, but he never once looked up from his paper. Except once, when he slid his cup of coffee across the table and his saucer collided with mine. Some of the coffee ran into the saucer and made a moat. Sorry, he said, and glanced up. It's nothing, I wanted to say, but he was already entering another word into the crossword of the folded newspaper alongside his plate. On the way back to the office I bought a magazine and read the love story at odd times through the afternoon when there was nothing to do, The heroine was like me but it had a happy ending, or, at least, where the story stopped. It was already dark outside, long before it was time to finish and go home. The woman at the switchboard was knitting a pullover for her husband. She liked a good joke. After a few days had gone by he rang me: could he see me? Had I changed my mind? Yes, I said, come over, and started to cry. He could hear something odd about my voice over the line. It's nothing, I said, hopeless tears running down my face. This is a very bad line he said, and hung up.

I prayed for a terrible accident, to make things bleed. Perhaps the roses will begin to open in the warmth of this room, drop a petal. Perhaps I would be able to scream. Nothing happened. I've ordered the cake, said my mother. You'd better start thinking about a guest list.

The nurse entered the room with a tray. They've got some special cakes, she said. I've brought you one with a cherry. The cake had been poured into fluted paper and baked. One candied cherry was stuck on top, marooned in a patch of pink icing. She was watching me. I tried to smile. I picked up the teacup and the liquid looked purplish in the artificial light. I put it down. A hair crack ran down the side. Perhaps it was a hair. I did not know how to explain myself. The nurse was still looking at me.

I did not know how to explain myself: to myself. As far as everybody else was concerned explanations were not required. I suddenly found myself, for the first and only time in my life, playing the lead. Everybody else played a supporting role, by which I mean, they supported me, handed me down the line like a giant parcel in a game of which I had no previous knowledge. They took charge, propelled me forward. My mother took me to the shops to look at bedlinen. I pleaded tiredness but it did not work. Only six weeks to go, she warned, and you can't start life without the basic necessities. What sort of sheets did I want, she asked, standing at the counter, candy stripes or plain white? I shrugged and said: white, I suppose. It was what I had always been used to. She conducted me down to the basement to look at saucepans. You'll need at least two frying-pans, she said. No good starting with less. The girls at the office had clubbed together to buy me a set of tablemats, and my future in-laws had already promised a cutlery service. Now, she said, turning away from the saucepan section, you'll be needing an ironing board. What kind were you thinking of?

I sit up in bed now as my mother once sat. Dry bits of cake crumble in my mouth. I must try to swallow them. She sat wrapped up in wool, a pink shell-pattern bedjacket I had made for her. The thread enmeshed me too, hour after hour, we could neither of us get out of the tangle. The nurses admired the delicate work.

My daughter brought me a clean nightgown last night. I am now wearing it. Although she had a busy day she did not forget. She must have spent a good deal of her spare time washing and ironing on my behalf. She is a good girl. Last night she was unduly worried about the condition of her grandmother, who had an accident yesterday. It must have been a bad day, rather worse than usual. And I am anxious that she should not overtax her strength. Adolescence is trying enough.

She has, of course, a particular link with her grandmother. I had forgotten that. Lying here, I have allowed so much to slip my mind, but I remember now that I found it hard at times, the way she managed to usurp my rightful place. Not from any sinister motive, she was only doing her best in a difficult situation, for which, as she was quick to remind me, I had only myself to blame. But I realized that she had found a new sense of purpose, for the first time in years perhaps, since my brother had left home. She knew all about diet and toilet training, nothing anybody could tell her about child-rearing, and since I was now back at my old job I hardly ever saw her

during the day. I did not like the job any more than I did
before I got married but it was steady, secure, and anyway
there was nothing else I could do, and I had the child to think
of now. By the time I got back at the end of the day she would
be tucked up in bed, asleep most likely. She had the child's
day nicely organized. Don't go in, she'd say, as I stood, still in
my coat, with my hand ready to turn the doorknob, I've just
got her settled. She needs her sleep. Her aggrieved tone
implied that if I disturbed her now I would undo a whole
day's work, and it was trying enough for a woman of her
years. We've had quite a day of it today, she told me over a
cold supper. Little madam didn't want to eat her lunch. Then
she played in the garden and got herself covered in mud.
Such a shame. That new dress I bought her only last week.
She nearly screamed the house down when I brought her in
and gave her a bath.

This was what I had come home for, stood wearily at the bus
stop in the cold and dark, jostled body to body, after a tedious
day during which I had scarcely spoken to anybody. And I
had to be grateful. Well, she said, I warned you. As you make
your bed so you must lie. And a child needs a father. On your
head be it.

I watched anxiously for symptoms. He called at the door to
take her to the park, sometimes the zoo. She thought he was
an uncle, but he came quite regularly. He stood on the door-
step until she came out in her coat. See she doesn't lose them,
I said, meaning her gloves. It was a sharp frosty day. Unspoken words hung between us. Once my mother asked him
to come in and he stepped over the threshold and sat uneasily
on the edge of a chair whilst she poured cups of tea. He had
unbuttoned his raincoat but did not take it off. I avoided his
eyes. The words had gummed up my mouth with round hard
pebbles. At all costs I wanted to avoid choking.

Please do not ask questions: that was what my face tried to express. At all costs let us avoid a useless scene. After all, I had not asked you any questions.

I had stood for what seemed hours, stood at the window, idle, looking down at the dead road, nobody moving, nobody moving in or out of their houses. The stillness of bated breath, unnatural, it could not go on, that was what I felt, surely something must crack, an unknown catastrophe, but it did go on. The house behind me was a hollow, a network of empty spaces. The baby had been put down hours ago. I had nothing to do. The telephone had not rung: there had been no message. Someone had cast a spell on the entire world, a pall of silence. I did not know what to do. I left the bedroom and began to walk down the flight of stairs. On the landing I paused outside the baby's room, my ear to the door. Silence. I went down the rest of the stairs and turned into the kitchen. I heard a hiss of gas, smelled an odour. His meal had been left to simmer several hours ago. I lifted the lid: the casserole so thoughtfully prepared had now burned dry, bits of charred meat stuck to the bottom of the pan. I opened the back door and scraped the contents into the dustbin. I glanced up and saw two stars in the strip of night sky between two houses. I flung the dish on to the hard ground.

Come along, he told the child. Are you ready? He placed the empty cup back in its saucer, carefully. That was very nice, he said to her, meanwhile trying to catch my eye. I avoided it.

Everything went on as usual. Or it seemed to. After all, I never asked you any questions. You must have thought that very convenient. It occurred frequently now, or at least, more often. The pauses got longer, the silences. I stood at the window many times, out of boredom, not waiting for anything.

89

Unless it was for the moment when the storm would finally break.

You left me alone. I pretended to be asleep by the time you came into the bedroom. You did not ask me about my day, since each day was as uneventful as the last. As for your life, I only heard what you wanted to tell me. It must have been a relief for you, that I did not press you, since you always came home extremely tired. It was a hard life, but you were reasonably good about money, and pleased as the baby made progress. You must have felt very secure. You came and went as you pleased. I expect you often congratulated yourself on your choice of a wife.

I had stood looking down at the dead road for hours. Husbands had come home, swinging through small gates with their briefcases. Now the street was deserted. There was nothing for me to do. The day had been like all the other days, shopping, cleaning, cooking, in the hours between feeding and changing the baby. I was not waiting for anything. The telephone would not ring. I had not asked questions, because all my life I had known what to expect. The taxi drew up at the gate. I put on my coat and left the bedroom. On the landing I went into the child's room and picked her up. Two suitcases stood waiting in the hall. I opened the front door and the driver took them to his cab. But I did not go just like that. Oh no. Fair's fair. I checked the oven once more and left a note on the kitchen table: YOUR DINNER IS IN THE OVEN.

12

The day is drawing to a close. It is evening now. The whole building shudders, vibrates to the sound of homeward traffic. Nobody has come. The chair stands, as it has always stood, with its back across the far left-hand corner.

My body has been washed, the bedclothes smoothed. I lie, waiting. There is, I now realize, nothing to wait for. Except, perhaps, a conclusion. Which will complete the pattern, like a jigsaw puzzle. Everything will fall into place, and I shall realize how much time I wasted, struggling to make things fit, looking at things from the wrong angle.

The tap above the washbasin still makes a gasping sound, like a dying person fighting for breath. This morning I might have thought of a hissing swan. Nurse, when she tipped away the dirty soapy water, must have forgotten to twist it off tight.

I have not been much good at putting things together. I tried hard enough, but I was inclined to suspect that the suppliers had slipped up, or perhaps it was my own fault that something was lost, missing. I would get down on the floor, fumbling in the half darkness, running my fingers along surfaces. I do not know what I expected to find.

My temperature and pulse rate have been taken once more. The chart of my progress through this particular dimension. It hangs at the foot of my bed, facing outward, so I am unable to see it. I therefore know nothing about the immediate situation. Only that at some stage the staggering line, wandering like the outline of foothills seen from a moving train, will pass off the page.

Oh, said my mother. You've finished it. I did not know what to do with the puzzle, which could now only be broken up.

A visitor, should somebody come, would be able to read the chart for me. But it is a condition of entry that such people are sworn to silence. Otherwise they are not allowed in.

I have studied the chair so long that it has begun to resemble some sort of monument, a statue. A stiffened lap figure in a perpetual sitting posture, arms deprived of hands, extensions of wood which are able to accept but not touch, not hold, not grasp. The eternal figure with brave shoulders but no head. Mother, woman, as man has carved her out of wood or stone.

No hands to hold, no feet with which to run. The broad lap becomes a springboard. Always the child is seen perched on the very edge, leaning forward, smiling, hands outstretched to grab the world in his greedy little fists. His baby prick dangles between his legs.

The chair remains behind, rigid, static. It was only a chair anyway. It cannot change or be changed.

The nurse has rubbed my buttocks so that I will not develop bedsores. It is too late for me to move, after all this time. You must become a chair, said my mother, pushing my brother forward. Help me to push, she told me, since he was somewhat unwilling, had no intention of going in any particular direction, did not know where he wanted to go. My mother had decided to push him up the steps of the institution, and this meant both of us putting all our weight behind him. He was lazy, kept wanting to roll back down. Later we walked up the flight of shallow steps, through the massive portico with its Doric columns to watch him receive his diploma. We sat in the audience and applauded. My mother had treated me to a new hat for the ceremony, so that he could feel proud of us too, when he returned from the platform in his new gown and spoke a few words to us.

He'll be all right now, she said, he'll be able to make a good living, as we came home on the underground. He had gone off to celebrate with some friends.

I wonder how much the roses cost? Not enough.

How beautiful, say the nurses, touching them lightly with the tips of their fingers, putting a nose forward to sniff. But shop roses have no scent. They comment: you are a lucky girl.

I never saw the card. Somebody's secretary picked up the telephone, having been told. Or perhaps she reminded him. Roses are so suitable.

The nurses put their fingers to the wounds and say: how pretty.

Some of the men wore hoods lined with scarlet satin, draped across their shoulders above the black gowns. My brother had one of pale blue. Some of the hoods were trimmed with fur, denoting a higher income bracket. My brother made a down-payment on a second-hand car and disappeared.

The nurses put their noses to the wounds and inhale, deeply. Imagining the perfume they ought to have.

He drove dangerously, which worried my mother, and at times still had the bewildered look I had known in him as a boy.

Won't you tell me, sis? he asked. What's the matter? I could not answer. He brought toys for the child. What's the good of it, said my mother, stacking the dirty dishes on the table, no good raking over the ashes. I looked down at my hands, twisting and turning nervously in my lap. What's done is done, so what's the point of talking about it. Though she knows what I think. And she picked up the pile of used plates and walked through the open door into the kitchen.

Men in white coats probe the wounds with sharp instruments, folding back the soft, bruised petals.

I do not earn enough, but I pride myself on making ends meet. She has never gone without anything. I have seen to that. The child that sat in my lap. I will give her a push. Forward.

He came to the door to collect her and I made sure the child was wearing her best clothes, everything neat and clean. Hair brushed. He should not be able to say anything against me. He said he would bring her back by six, her bed and supper time when she was small. I don't understand you, she said, after the door had closed. The empty house was already closing in on an empty afternoon. Please don't, mother, I answered: I don't wish to discuss it. And I went upstairs to lie down. Perhaps his wife had the flowers sent. She always knew about the child's birthday, had a gift for her.

Sometimes I was afraid she would be seduced by the gifts. She would come back and describe the house. It was so comfortable, with a room just for her. He could afford it. I have not had a pay rise for several years. I know, though I say nothing, that some of the younger girls just out of school are getting as much or even more than me. But I say nothing. I take a pride in making ends meet. I have always managed so far. Soon my child will leave home. My own needs are very small. I have no appetites. Nowadays I am not even hungry.

The old woman has brought in my supper. She smiles her artificial smile, showing an arc of false teeth, and slides the tray on to the locker. Her body smells of washing-up water. Some kind of mush, coloured bright yellow with artificial breadcrumbs. Eat it up, dearie—visiting time soon. She leaves the room slowly, hobbling on her bad foot. Evening becomes palpable, the night drawing in. I can hardly see the branch across the window. Outside it will soon be quite dark. Inside the white light is bluish, which makes the food look un-appetizing, gives things a curious tinge, so that yellow looks shrill, dentures false. Suppers is served early here, as though I were back in childhood. But the food does not look whole-some; nor will our sleep, later, be wholesome.

The mashed potato makes a noise in my mouth. I can feel hard lumps between tongue and palate. Glued, or threatening to choke if I swallow. I move my jaw slowly, hearing the noise between my ears. I do not know whether the croquette is of fish or fowl, under the layer of yellow crumbs. My eye has already begun to study the pudding which stands waiting, in a side plate, suspiciously. It is white, has a curious sheen, bluish as shivering flesh. It has been tipped out of a mould. I do not like the look of it. Nevertheless, I shall attempt to eat it.

13

She (I) came into the room and kissed me (her) on the cheek, bending down over the bed. Her face felt fresh and cool from the winter evening outside. (Her warm face felt dry, almost desiccated to my touch.) How are you, mother? I felt my age: looking at her. She was looking youthful, her face flushed from the cold air, and smart, in the dark blue coat I had bought her several weeks ago. (I always wanted to look nice.) And she was breathing hard as though she had been running, down the long corridors and up the stairs. Whew, she said, I'm puffed. I was afraid I'd be late. (I pulled up the chair and sat down to get my breath back. Now I saw that she was looking dreadful: her head on the pillow had shrunk, the slackened skin had grown new lines, its pallor only muted by a deadness of texture. She had a listless air, limp strands of hair strewn on the supporting pillow. Something about the mouth and eyelids.)

You shouldn't have rushed, I said. What's the difference? I'm used to it, waiting.

I know, she said. But I didn't want you to think I wasn't coming. I just missed a bus and then I had to wait for ages. There were lots of people waiting and all the buses seemed to be the wrong number, or full up.

You're a good girl, I said.

(I know what it's like, she said, you shouldn't have rushed.)

You shouldn't have rushed, I said, I know you've got a lot of things to do.

She was opening her coat and I saw her firm young legs with

approval. Under it she had on a brightly flowered dress.
You're looking very nice.

Thanks. She smiled. But how about you? How are you feeling? What do the doctors say?

(She shrugged: I don't know. I suppose it takes time. It's not
too bad. Funny how one gets used to the days here.)

I shrugged.

How is everybody?

She appeared not to have heard. I've brought you a clean
nightgown, she said.

(I began to unwrap the package, trying hard to avoid the
questions she was waiting to ask.)

Shall I bring you something to read?

I shook my head.

(I can't seem to concentrate, somehow, she sighed.)

Funny how the time passes, I said. That's a pretty dress.

Do you like it? She sounded relieved. I thought maybe I'd
make another one, the same as this, only in a plain material, or
perhaps with pleats down the back and a large belt. What do
you think? She had taken off her coat, flung it across the back
of the chair, and now stood with her back half-turned towards
the bed, looking over her shoulder in my direction.

A lot of work, I said.

I know, she said, and sat down with a sigh. I think it's too
difficult.

What about school? I asked. That's much more important.

She shrugged: I don't know.

I want to push you up the steps of the institution.

Mother! What are you talking about?

I mean it. Your whole future is at stake.

(I was in no mood to think about homework. I was still breathless, hoped my flushed face would not give me away.)

What have you been doing, just now, in the corridor?

Nothing. (I flushed a deeper scarlet.) I told you why I was
late. I've been running, I'm still out of breath.

(I could see she did not believe me.)

What have you been up to?

Nothing! Honestly, mother, I do like school. It's just that I can't seem to concentrate at the moment.

Other things on your mind.

Maybe.

(Her hands, having cooked a thousand meals, scrubbed the remnants out of as many pots and pans, remade beds, tucking in sheets and bedding day after day, now lay resting on the bedspread, the right hand lightly holding on to the left hand, still grimly distinguished by the gold band, worn now, dull, the knuckle had swollen over the years and nobody could get it off, they would have to bury her with it. She had joked about that often enough, though now it was no longer a joke. She could not laugh anyhow, because the stitches hurt. She pulled a grimace as she tried to shift further up the bed. Shall I help you? She shook her head. I began to unwrap the package.)

Shall I put it in your locker?

The future, I said, you must think about your future.

She screwed up the paper and came close to the bed.

Is there somewhere I can put this?

She glanced round.

I took hold of her wrist. She was still standing close to the bed.

Is something the matter?

Her face, I saw now, looked anxious, had a tense expression.

(I did not try to pull my hand away but avoided the query in her eyes.)

No, of course not. Goodness, what beautiful roses.

(Why has nobody come to see me, she burst out suddenly. Why? Why?)

She sniffed at the roses.

They have no scent, I commented. Don't pretend.

Did father send you these?

(Why? Why?)

I don't know. Perhaps you can tell me.

How should I know. Honestly, mother, I hardly ever see him

nowadays. He's constantly on the road, never back for more than a few hours. But he said to tell you he'd be in to see you just as soon as he could spare the time.

That's good of him.

(She let go of my arm, as though she was not strong enough to go on grasping it. Her face looked sunken, with hollow eyes and greyish skin. She's going to need a long convalescence, he had told me, outside in the corridor. Is that going to be possible?)

You're keeping something from me. What is it?

(I shook my head, looking thoughtfully at the stethoscope slung round his neck. I'll see what I can arrange, he said.)

No, they don't smell, do they. But they look beautiful, all the same. She touched one curved petal with the tip of her finger. Perhaps he did send them. I was dozing when the nurse brought them in, so I never saw the card.

You see.

(I answered absentmindedly. I could still see his eyes on my face. He was being exceptionally sympathetic and kind.)

I could see she was keeping something from me.

Well?

He didn't say much. Let's talk about you first.

There's nothing to talk about.

Oh, come on, mother. The doctors must have told you something.

Well, I said, not wanting to talk about it, they don't seem too sure what to do with me. But today he sounded quite optimistic.

Good.

Though I don't know what about.

But surely, by this time, they must know . . .

Don't worry about it, please darling. You haven't told me anything yet.

(I could not avoid the moment much longer. Perhaps she had already guessed. I said that my brother was fine but that he had so much homework, still, he had promised to come in with me at the weekend. I laughed, but the laugh was forced. He needed a haircut. Perhaps I'll try and get him to a barber first. And your father?)

And your father? I said out loud. It was out, but I had only been speaking from memory.

She looked down at me, and I could read the unease in her normally frank eyes, the wish to escape.

I've already told you.

What did you tell me?

He's all right.

There was a prolonged silence. She volunteered no more information.

He's very worried about you.

Sure.

No, really. I thought perhaps he had sent you the flowers.

He might have come.

(Go in and talk to her now, he had said. But be careful what you say. She's still very weak. He put his hand on my shoulder, comfortingly, like an elder brother. I had an impulse to blurt everything out. I wanted to burst into tears. I was afraid that I would.)

He's been away a lot recently.

It's none of my business. Don't bother to explain.

But he told me to tell you: just as soon as he's got a moment he'll be in to see you. He's very worried about you.

So you said.

But he's working very hard just now. He's hardly got into town and he has to leave again, go off somewhere else.

You already told me.

She kept staring at the crumpled ball of paper in her hands, squeezing it, now she was chewing her lower lip.

Poor child, I thought, but then I became suspicious: what had the doctor told her?

What did he say to you outside?

Who?

The doctor.

Nothing. I didn't see anybody.

(Her eyes, those two black holes, stared across the room at me. Inside she now had a third hole, and it was devouring her, eating her up with the days. So her flesh had sunk with the growing hollow inside. The look in her eyes was a hungry look, that was it.)

After a pause, she had now tossed the crumpled paper into the corner of the room, she continued: Are you eating? Is the food dreadful? Would you like me to bring you in some fruit?

I shook my head. I've no appetite.

(She shook her head wearily, as though to say: stop it. I know you're keeping something from me. She may even have said: you lose all interest in food here, it's the lack of activity.)

Something's the matter, isn't it, I asked gently. My poor lamb. She flushed suddenly, an angry scarlet, and I saw drops of water sparkle in both eyes. But she shook her head.

It's awful to be young, I said.

She wiped her eyes with the back of her hand. It's nothing.

(I'm sorry, she said. Lying here all day, I start to imagine things. She blew her nose and wiped both eyes with the back of her hand. I get so depressed. Now you're being silly, I said. You'll soon be home, and well. But you're not helping yourself by crying. She grimaced with pain as she tried to lift herself higher in the bed. I'm being idiotic. She made an attempt at a hollow laugh.)

She walked across the room and sat down on the chair which had been waiting.

I hate men.

It was like a thought coming out of one's own head. (Watching her attempting to laugh, the pain etched into her face, I hated him. I gripped the wooden arms to control myself.)

You mustn't do that.

Her face was still flushed. She was an attractive child, but now, with so much expression, colour suffusing the skin, she had a momentary, angry beauty.

You mustn't do that I said kindly, watching her across the

room, hunched on the edge of the chair, nibbling now at her nails. I think you should forget about me, leave home, make a life for yourself. You could travel perhaps, go abroad. Would you like to do that?

She shrugged.

There must be something you would like to do. Or study?

I don't know.

Or take the chance while you're young and travel.

Where?

I don't know. Lots of places.

(I've never heard such nonsense, she scolded. I wouldn't dream of letting you go. I don't know what Maureen's parents think they are doing. Italy of all places, that's no place for young girls to be gadding about on their own. How would you live? It's none too clean I hear, and you've no idea, those Latins don't leave women alone.)

I don't know, I said. Lots of places. What about Italy?

What about it?

She stared at me, unconvinced, as though she had never quite seen me before. I could see the sun dazzling on blue water, the bright outline of white buildings against an arc of flawless sky. White doves rising in a flock. The sound of bells, frescoes peeling. The sun, the sun on my back, face and neck. My body alive with it. I would like to imagine her walking, her strong young body moving between the white buildings that reflected light, perhaps not walking alone, she was holding somebody's hand, but I could not see what he looked like, it was just a hand. Her arms and legs were quite brown.

Yes, she said. I'll think about it. Only . . .

Only what?

Granny's X-ray has come through. It's a fracture, a bad one. The doctor has been talking to me about it. That's why I was late. He said we must expect a long job, considering her age. And of course she's agitating to come home. You know granny, how she fusses. And there's been nobody to come and see her the whole day. Apparently she cried.

The white building shattered into sharp fragments. It was impossible to walk forward, each shard might prove fatal.

You must get in touch with your uncle.

One slip, it only took one slip, a careless moment, one foot put wrong. I knew. I had seen it happen before. And so, in fact, had she.

I should have been there, I said. It's my fault. If I had been at home it might never have happened.

Don't be silly.

You don't know. You're too young. Old bones don't heal easily. My grandmother went like that. Probably that was why she cried.

You mustn't worry. Apparently it's her stomach she's chiefly complaining about. You know how she's been going on about her stomach for the past few months. They told her they'd do some tests, in a day or two, when she's better.

I should have been there, I said. Marvellous old woman, your mother, they used to comment, never complaining, keeping the house just so, the secret would die with her, or so she thought. She was too proud to show any pain.

I must get up. I must come home.

But how can you? Don't worry about it, mother. I was afraid you would fret. I'll go in to see her. I'll take time off school if necessary. You know granny, how she fusses, she was always like that. She'll be as right as rain. In no time.

Your uncle.

I think he has gone away for a few days. On business.

He is her son. But he will say that he cannot stand sick rooms, that he has to catch up on his homework. He will come eventually, with a bunch of flowers and say How are you, mother? But he will not stop to take off his coat. He will pace up and down, and the chair will remain empty, waiting. The visitor's chair. People need company when they are dying. They should not be left alone, to study the blank walls, staring intermittently at the empty chair, deprived of reassuring words.

Go home now, I said. You look tired. You've had a long day. There were dark smudges under her eyes. Her young face looked drawn with the effort of keeping up appearances, coping with new emotions, invisible forces still not understood, and the physical strain of growing.

It's all right, she mumbled. I'm all right.

Off you go, I said. It's late. And anyhow, I'm tired too.

I put on an expression of weariness, playing the invalid with some skill. She got up abruptly and walked towards the bed, towards me, with renewed vigour, a sudden freshness.

I'm *so* sorry, mother. I hadn't thought.

She leaned down towards my head and I saw a tiny woman's head, white, distant, repeated twice over in the two pupils before she came closer and out of focus. Her warm flesh brushed against mine. The pressure of the soft mouth was moist. Such contact, what would I not give for such contact. The touch of this flesh was life. My daughter.

Good night, mother. I'll see you tomorrow. Sleep well.

14

I could see her walk down the staircase, pausing on the landing, going on down the next flight. Her footsteps would echo on the tiled floor as she walked through the wide entrance hall with its columns at the door.

I lie alone in the small white room.

Coming through the heavy doors, walking between the grey columns to stand, for a moment, looking down from the first of a flight of shallow steps, the clamour would hit her, the din, a chaos of heavy traffic, engines revving, brakes screeching, the irritable sound of hooters, headlights flashing, signals blinking, move forward, turn left, red stop, green go, bluish neon lights on long thin stalks drooping heads, casting an aura on stone façades. Above it all a blanket of dark silence. Ignored.

I lie alone in the small white room. In a sense I shall continue to lie within it, always. There is no way of leaving it.

Unless I pass through the door. In which case I shall carry it with me, in my head.

She walked down the flight of steps and, without hesitating, turned left and walked along the pavement towards the bus stop. She has done it so often, it has already become a habit. She takes her place in a line of dark figures become shapeless inside bundles of clothes. Each person stands facing the back of the person in front. Young or old, man or woman, since each shadow stands with his back turned to those behind, it does not matter, the point of sensitivity between the shoulder-blades, how close the face, almost touching, but frozen with the night air, squinting now towards the most distant visible point of the road, almost a grimace, waiting for the vehicle illuminated with the correct number so that one will soon be homeward bound.

It has all been a valuable experience.

She did not see the doctor again before leaving the building. Though she hesitated at the top of the stairs. And again on the lower landing. She was anxious to speak to him, but nobody appeared. The building suddenly seemed oddly deserted as she stood in the corridor, looking down its aseptic length. After a few such moments a nurse came out through a door, saw her standing uncertainly and smiled: could she help her? What did she want? Was she, possibly, lost? No. She shook her head. Thanks all the same. And she started to walk down the staircase, hurriedly.

Standing now in a silent line of humans, cold, in the dark, the unanswered questions hung heavily in the air above her head. They seemed to account for the weariness of her shoulders, the way they now sagged. And for the hollow space, the gnawing hunger that grew inside her.

But she was still very young. The appearance of a bus, like a promise at the end of the road, the activity of trying to read whether it was the correct route number and, having established that it was, of trying not to lose her place in the queue and, more than that, pushing and shoving in the crowd to get on it, all this made her forget, for a moment, both her own weariness and the dull ache inside. She brushed the queries aside, dispelled, momentarily, the sense of aura which hung like a bluish haze above her own head and the whole city. The bus looked warm inside, it was lit up. It would take her home. She began to move.

15

I knew every detail of the road by heart. Coming from the bus stop, past the tobacconist on the corner, I turned into the dimly lit network of small roads behind. It was always the same, day in, day out, the box hedges, neatly cut, or grown ragged and about to be neatly cut, the small gates of wood or wrought iron, thus aspiring to individuality, each opening on to short straight paths to doors identical in all but colour. It was the pretention to grandeur that I disliked most, I positively hated the fancy patterns of wrought iron and imitation coach lamps. It made the other houses look so shabby, which was, I felt, the intention.

I had known this suburban world all my life, had grown up in it, and yet it was not coming home at all. I had never felt as though I belonged in it, as though this was a place to which one could belong. I did not know the people who lived in the houses on the other side of the road, we did not know anybody. We exchanged polite nods with our immediate neighbours, and avoided meeting unless we had to. My mother thought them vulgar, what she called ill-educated.

In my mind's eye the roads formed a grid, in which we lived: trapped. Roads, I thought in my childish fashion, ought to lead somewhere, to a centre, a meeting place where everybody gathered at foreknown times and occasions. Perhaps I was influenced by my history lessons, but I liked the idea of the village at the crossroads, the church with its spire, and bells ringing out messages. I drew maps of it in my exercise book, and imagined what it must have been like, living so. It would be pleasant, under the old trees, the hours marked off by the sun's arc, a day's journey. But this, here the roads led nowhere, only to more roads, exactly similar, with identical houses, sprawling across a flat land without demarcations except an arterial road, a row of shops, and the local cinema. Which in turn led on to another network of sleepy roads, drugged houses, dead occupants.

Coming up from the bus stop, past the tobacconist on the corner with the board of small ads, it was always the same: very quiet, rows of privet hedges boxing in the patches of front garden, light glowing from several windows. But most of the curtains had already been drawn, through the windows one could see just a strip of bright light, a gap in the curtains which hinted at the warmth inside from which the passerby was excluded. Lamps, a drinks cabinet, soft carpets and ugly chairs. It was a privacy that made me want to laugh, because all the houses were the same inside, the interiors identical, they made a great fuss about drawing their curtains and shutting their front doors against me but I knew the shape of their kitchen and which door on the upstairs landing led to the bathroom.

Number thirty-one.

I lifted the latch of the wooden gate, pushed back the gate, with difficulty, because the hedge needed trimming, and walked up the garden path. All the windows looked dead, dark. I pushed my doorkey into the lock and turned, inside the hall lay in darkness, I could hear nothing, but saw a thin strip of yellow light under the kitchen door. The light switch was by the living-room door, on the left opposite the stairs, but I knew my way well enough. I walked through the darkness, still in my outdoor coat, and opened the door into the kitchen.

My brother was sitting on a kitchen stool, legs akimbo, heels hooked into the wooden rung below. He held a paper dart poised in his hand, between me and his right ear. He had been about to propel it across the room. Instead he turned his head round and looked at me. Hi, sis. You're late. Father isn't here. I'm fed up with waiting for you both.

Have you eaten?

I took off my coat and looked at the dirty cups, plates and knives. An open jam-jar stood on the table, Crumbs everywhere. I went back into the hall, switched on the light, and hung my coat on the stand near the telephone table. The hall ceiling was decorated with false beams, stained to look like old oak. A small window by the door was leaded with a pattern of stained glass. The telephone stood just below it.

Not really. I had some tea. But I was waiting for you. I thought nobody would ever come. It was boring.

Has father rung?

No.

I came back into the kitchen. He was now flinging the paper dart across the room. It jammed in the plate rack above the cooker.

Come on, I said, picking up plates, cups and spoons from the table and stacking them in the sink. Help me to clear this mess and I'll make us both an omelette.

Ugh. You know I don't like omelettes.

I can't help that. It's late and I'm tired. Anyhow, it's quick. You want to eat now, don't you, not at midnight?

Oh, all right. He got off the stool and took knives and forks out of the cutlery drawer. But what about father?

Damn father. I don't care about father.

He retrieved his dart from the plate rack. Are you in a bad mood?

No. Just tired.

He flung the dart upward so that it hit the ceiling and did a nosedive into the linoleum. He still liked war games, but I had long understood that all pilots were only flesh and blood. I pulled back the larder door.

Everything has gone funny, hasn't it, since mother went into hospital? I don't like it at home now. I wish she would come back. Why does father stay out so late?

I said nothing. The white shells felt very cold and smooth in my hands. I smashed each egg against the rim of the mixing bowl. One. Two. Three. The liquid oozed out, viscous. The small suns of future days. I smashed the floating yolks with my fork.

He was sitting on the stool again. He had begun to chew his nails, a habit he had.

She'll be back soon. Only the doctor says she's going to need a long convalescence first. I don't know how we'll manage.

Does that mean she's not getting better?

No, I said, above the noise of the sizzling pan, it just means it's going to be a slow business. It takes a long time to get over some illnesses.

In his eyes I had seen a momentary dread. Something new, as I cut the omelette in half and slid one portion on to his plate. He sat straddling the stool, clutching its rim with both hands. Eat your omelette. There was a word he could not say. Also, he was afraid his normal routine would be disturbed, or perhaps, who knows, his whole world smashed. It was a possibility he had not even considered till now.

She asked after you.

I'll go in and see her at the weekend. Honest I will. What have they done to her anyhow? He paused with the fork in his hand, egg on his lower lip. I don't understand.

Never mind.

Did I tell you, I've been chosen for the second eleven and today I was the only person who scored a goal.

Your supper's getting cold.

And I got top marks in the biology test.

That's good.

You know, sis, he said a little later, after we had finished eating. It's funny, being on our own like this, with dad out all the time and mum away. It's as though we'd never had any parents. Imagine growing up on your own, without any adults at all.

Would you like that?

I don't know. When I was small I used to think about being an orphan.

So did I.

But then I thought, what's the use. You'd get hungry and cold, and then somebody would take charge anyhow.

Yes.

So perhaps I'd rather have us. Unless we were the first people. Imagine living in a great big dark green jungle, with lots of fruit hanging on all the branches.

And spiders crawling about. And snakes. No thank you.

I laughed.

You wouldn't have to be frightened of snakes, he said. I'd kill them for you.

Thanks.

When they die, he said, do you think they'll leave us lots of money?

I don't know. What an awful thing to say.

Well, will they?

I don't know. Not lots. Some.

Yes, but how much?

I've no idea. Does it matter?

I'm saving up for a car.

You shouldn't think about such things. It's not nice. And you haven't finished your omelette.

I don't want it. I hate omelettes. You know I don't like omelettes.

The table was littered with dirty plates, knives and forks lying askew, surfaces smeared, a crust of bread, dregs of cold tea at the bottom of white cups. His short hair was rumpled, the school tie hung loose round his shirt collar, unbuttoned at the neck. In the bluish light of the kitchen she could not make up her mind whether his small face was smudged with dirt or if it was shadowed with fatigue. She knew that up above the house lay cold and empty, deserted spaces, dark. He would not, neither of them would want to go up. Go upstairs and have your bath, she said.

Oh but, he objected, dad isn't even home yet.

Go on, she said. Bed.

It's early, he had lied.

It's late, she had retorted, and by now he was too tired to argue. He lurched forward, off the stool, for a moment it looked as though he might stumble, fall head first. His pale skin looked positively bruised now, under the surface, beneath his eyes. He went towards the door.

It was later, much later, when he did come home. The car lights broke the darkened silence in which I had been sitting, for what seemed hours, my feet folded under me in the deep armchair, for warmth, looking round the dim room. I could just pick out the faint outline of furniture, how it stood, now that it was abandoned, unused, as it must always have stood, during the night hours. Upstairs my brother would be asleep by now, chasing his dreams. I thought about him with a touching new affection, curious, since we had always been separate, fighting, having quarrels, bitter rivals for attention. Apart from which, I was jealous of him, since I knew that I counted for nothing in my mother's eyes, being a girl, in comparison. And she had admitted it: that a son was something special. But he needed me now, lying half hidden under the bedclothes for protection. He was such a child.

I sat curled up in the chair, in the dark, listening to the hours pass. The curtains were drawn back. It was dark outside, and the car when it arrived caused a shaft of light to probe round the room. The engine died.

I heard his key in the door. Because I was sitting in the dark he did not know I was still up and awake. He was moving very quietly in the hall. I heard him switch on the light and whisper, or perhaps, mutter, to himself. He must have thought we were fast asleep upstairs, tucked up in our little beds. I heard him knock into a chair and curse quietly. Father? I said, going towards the door, feeling my way between the furniture in the dim room. Is that you? An absurd question. I suppose I had been waiting up for him, though I had not told myself this. I had simply sat down in the empty room, in the dark, with the curtains drawn back on the night, with a curious kind of clarity, a calm I had not felt before. If I was waiting, and I suppose I was, it was not so much because I wanted him home as because I wanted to involve him in what I was feeling. But meanwhile I had forgotten about him; sitting there by myself, thinking. It was such a curious experience, being alone, in the dark, with the world asleep all round, or uninhabited, the hush as I felt the deserted house dark above my head, the quiet road lit outside, coming dimly through the folds of the net curtains across the window, the folds not moving, with me, also, not moving. I heard myself breathe in and out in the dark.

I pulled open the living-room door and blinked in the yellow light. He was leaning against the newel post at the bottom of the staircase with one hand, whilst he pushed off his shoes with the other. Because he was leaning forward I could see the bald patch on top of his head. Normally, when he stood upright, he was much taller than me. He raised his head, startled, his face looked very flushed.

What on earth are you doing, he said, putting his socked foot cautiously down on the linoleum floor. Why aren't you in bed?

I might ask you the same question, I said coldly and was astonished at myself. What are you sneaking about for?

I'm not sneaking about, he said loudly, angrily, then suddenly lowered his voice. I didn't want to wake you, that's all.

I see.

I stood with my hand on the doorknob, twisting it round and round. It sounded and felt somehow loose, as though it might come away from the wood.

Go up to bed, he said. It's late.

I shook my head. He was examining the heels of the pair of shoes which now dangled in his hand, as though he might have trodden in something. There was absolutely nothing wrong with the shoes, we both knew that.

No, I said. I'm not sleepy. I've been sleeping badly the past few days. And I wanted to talk to you.

Talk to me? He stared straight at me now, with a startled expression. He seemed amazed that I could have anything to say. What about?

He came towards me, and now I retreated, backing into the room. You've been sitting in the dark, he said, following me into the room. He switched on the lamp, but not before he had stumbled across the room and drawn both curtains across the window. Shutting out the street.

Yes, I said. I was thinking.

Light spilled over the furniture, so it looked almost normal now, warm and cosy. The lamp standing guard over the sofa threw a dim circle of light on to the shadowed ceiling.

Thinking? he echoed. What about?

He could not fool me now, though he had apparently regained his composure. I had detected a rising note of anxiety in his voice.

Oh, I said, just . . . things.

He had flung himself into an armchair and crossed his legs, arms stretched out. He had recovered his paternal assurance now, watching me as I hesitated, whilst I was fast losing mine. A mocking smile crept across his face.

Is that what you wanted to talk to me about in the middle of the night?

I shrugged, looking down at the floor, muttered: I suppose so. At any moment he might become angry, forgetting his indulgent mood.

What is all this nonsense?

Now. It was now or never. I had to act.

You've been with her, haven't you? I blurted out, suddenly, my heart beginning to beat loud and fast. I nodded towards the door. Late one night I had seen them both in the hall. Looking down from the landing outside my room I had seen them embracing near the hatstand.

Her? Who's her? I don't know what you mean.

Oh yes you do, I said. And he did. He had flushed darkly, and not with rage at my impertinence. I hated her, and now him, with a venom inappropriate to what I had seen, I knew that. But it was her fault: she had made him behave as no father should. And he was weak, was to blame for the state my mother was in. He did not care, about her, or any of us. He had betrayed us.

You needn't worry, I said, I'm not going to tell mother. I tried to control my voice, sustain this level of icy sarcasm. I was conscious of putting on an act. In a film I had seen a wife confront her husband with his adultery in this manner, using just this tone. She's hardly in a fit state just now. By the way, you haven't asked how she is.

You haven't given me much chance, he said slowly. Well, how is she?

From my experience of films I knew this was the moment to press home one's advantage. The doctor says she is making only slow progress. He can't quite understand it. And he also says that she is going to need a long convalescence. And of course she keeps asking after you, or sometimes not asking, which is worse. Every time I go in. I've run out of excuses. You'll have to go in and see her. Make it up to her.

I thought I had now coped with the problem. Everything would now be as before. As though it had never happened.

But he had begun to pick at the upholstery of the chair, a nervous habit which irritated my mother. Mother is always telling you not to do that, I thought in my head, watching him. He suddenly seemed to have lost his sense of time, of how late it was, that we had to get to bed to wake up in the early morning.

Look, he said, and his tone was apologetic. I wasn't going to tell you this now. I wanted to put it off. But I can't go in to see your mother. The fact is, I'm leaving her. You'll have to cope somehow. Don't worry, I'll see about cash and so forth. You'll be all right. But I can't go in to see her, it would only make things worse. I don't expect you to understand. But I can't go in and pretend everything is normal, if I do she'll come back home and everything will be as before, or she'll try to pretend that it is, and we'll go on as before and I shall never get away. You've no idea, how could you, but your mother and I have not been exactly happy these past few years, we tried to keep it from you, while you were still growing up, but now I must have a chance, too, to do a bit of living before it's too late. You'll have to cope, tell her anything, just for the moment. Till she's back on her feet. But I can't go in myself and face her. She'd know something was wrong. You must see that.

16

I saw a lot of things. For the first time I saw how I had seen him, a few days later, pack his things and put suitcases of personal belongings in the car. I saw how I had coped with the situation. You're a good girl, he had said, and kissed me lightly on the cheek. I watched him walk down the drive. For the first time I saw the contortions it had brought me to: coping. In order to lie to my mother, without appearing to do so, until she was strong enough to inhabit her own story. In order to accommodate my own loss, so that I would, for the present, continue to function, since the comfort of others depended on it. I poured syrup on my brother's food, and honeyed words on everything, trying to mellow the situation. I tried to mellow my hate, I spun a cocoon round the stone that dug a pain between my ribs so I would not feel it, because if I had not done so everything would have come to a stop.

We continued this way for years. I twisted my body to accommodate the lies, the new shape that the house had taken now, since mother came home. She has never fully accepted the truth. We contorted ourselves to the lies. A person must be strong enough to inhabit his or her own story.

The lump of stone with its grey cocoon has become part of my anatomy. I knew how to cope with it, how to move so as to avoid a sudden sharp pain. But it still grew, the threads multiplied and threatened to engulf me. Eventually it was necessary to lie still, to discontinue all movement, so as to avoid agony.

It is night now. I lie awake but calm. Sleep will come soon enough. The light has been switched off, but the shadows have no terrors for me now. I know this room. I know its contours, how the walls touch the ceiling. Air fills out the room in the way my body fills out its skin. Opposite, the far window gleams mysteriously, near and yet so distant.

It could all have been different.

But this moment is still a realization, even if it is too late.

Can a moment, when it comes, come too late, being still now? All moments are now.

I place my feet on the floor, having swung my legs across and down from the bed. I have a sensation of ascending or perhaps descending a spiral. Which, I do not know. I am the spiral. I can feel the surface of floor touch the tip of one bare toe, now the entire surface of the floor, my foot. The room assumes dimensions, through which it is possible to move.

Very slowly, I slide off the edge of the bed and put my weight on both feet. For a moment it is unbearable. I stagger, holding on the bedrail. The moment passes.

There are things which have to be done.

Somebody else will have to do the living.

But first, there is dying. I shall be in attendance, telling the necessary lies. To give comfort, a function I have always understood.

I let go of the bedrail and begin to move forward, feeling my way along the length of the bed. I hope there are no obstructions along the floor. I cannot see it yet, nor could I see it whilst I was lying on the bed. Perhaps I shall fall. But the walls are familiar, and the objects held in tension between them, I can now make them out with increasing clarity as my eyes get used to the dark. And I am moving steadily closer to the window.

My body is light now. It is only my legs which lack strength, since I have not used them for a long time.

Now that I am near to the window I can see that it is clearly a square. The old man's arm is a branch that continues. In a moment I will be able to touch the frame, should I wish.

I could, I realize, have stopped to turn off, finally throttle that gasping tap.

Instead I have only one aim: to reach the chair, where I know it stands, in the far corner, waiting for a human shape to occupy it.

I clutch the wooden arm, move forward one more step, turn round and lower myself into it.

For a moment my vision is obscured. All things swim in front of my eyes, I try to blink away the confused shapes. Stars, waves, moving branches. I am breathing hard. Gradually my breathing becomes calmer. My body has stopped trembling.

Across the room I see the bed. For the first time I see the entire fourth wall behind it, the bed as an object, its four legs poised on the floor on unsteady wheels, not rooted into it.

I am familiar with the contours of the room. Through the shadows I can make out the indented shape of the pillows, how they gleam faintly in the dark. The room is strangely quiet. I am breathing quietly, occupying the chair, my arms resting on the arm rests, feeling the cool firm wood under my palms. But I am not alone. In the bed, on the pillows that gleam white through the dark room, I can see the face of an old woman, lying with eyes closed, her skin the colour of sheets, sunk like a sheet draped over the profile of old sharp bones. I think she has stopped breathing, but perhaps she will continue for a little longer. I am waiting to hear if she has anything more to say. In any case I must continue to sit here until the breathing stops.